CELG

NO TIME FOR SECOND BEST

When Ellie Chapman finds out that she's inherited her Great-aunt Hilary's farm on the beautiful Kentish coast, and is then made redundant from her office job, it looks like life has handed her the new start she's been craving. But there are choppy waters ahead, from difficulties with her ex-fiancé, to the unexpectedly dilapidated state of the farm, to a menagerie with a poorly donkey and a wayward sheep. Love is waiting in the wings for both Ellie and her mum, however, as well as some exciting new opportunities . . .

JO BARTLETT

NO TIME FOR SECOND BEST

Complete and Unabridged

LINFORD
Leicester

First published in Great Britain in 2015

First Linford Edition
published 2016

A catalogue record for this book is available
from the British Library.

ISBN 978–1–4448–3017–0

Published by
F. A. Thorpe (Publishing)
Anstey, Leicestershire

Set by Words & Graphics Ltd.
Anstey, Leicestershire
Printed and bound in Great Britain by
T. J. International Ltd., Padstow, Cornwall

This book is printed on acid-free paper

1

'Are you planning to push that button, or just stop everyone else getting off?' A man's voice broke into Ellie's daydream and she dragged her eyes away from the poster advertising holidays on the south coast to look at him.

'Sorry?' It took a moment for her vision to adjust, but as he finally came into sharp focus, there was no doubt the impatience was directed at her. His face was blotchy and there was a muscle pulsing in his cheek. Maybe he'd had to stand up all the way from London, like she had; it was enough to make anyone grumpy.

'I asked if you're going to press that button when the train stops, because some of us have homes to go to and I don't want to be stuck on here any longer than I have to.' As he spoke, the train lurched to a halt and yellow lights illuminated the 'open door' button.

'Yes, of course. Sorry.' Mumbling a second apology as the doors slid open, Ellie offered a smile, but the man had already pushed past her, snagging his briefcase on her tights as he did so. Fighting the urge to say something about manners costing nothing, she followed him through the open doors, catching her breath as she stepped onto the platform. There was that same holiday advertisement — a meadow alive with wildflowers perched high on the cliffs, with a view across the English Channel — plastered across one of the station billboards.

'It could almost be Aunt Hilary's place.' The thought had been running through her head on the train and now she'd actually said it out loud. A teenage girl turned round, giving her a funny look. Ellie stared down at her feet until she was sure that the girl had moved on, and then looked back up at the poster. Since her great-aunt had died a few weeks before, memories of

Channel View Farm were occupying her thoughts more than ever. She hadn't been there in years — at least not to the house, and the realisation that she never would again weighed more heavily than the oversized handbag slung across her shoulder, the strap of which had been cutting into her skin since Victoria station. Did she really need all the things she lugged around with her? Yes, there were a lot of essentials, like her phone and laptop, but she still wasn't sure what she was supposed to do with the surprisingly weighty zip-up bag of overpriced cosmetics languishing in the bottom of her handbag. Rupert had bought them for her; apparently the women in his office swore by them. So she'd accepted his generous gift, despite it not really being her thing.

Ellie's stomach gave a loud grumble as she left the station, probably in protest at having missed lunch again. What was that old business mantra? *Lunch is for wimps.* Of course she hadn't really given up lunch for work; it had just been the lesser of two evils. It was either give up lunch or give up the daily treat of coming home to a slice of whatever cake her mother had baked. Just lately the waistbands of her work suits had started to leave angry red marks on her skin, and Rupert had made a comment about her getting 'cuddly', which she was almost certain wasn't a compliment. Then there was the wedding to think of, though lately she'd thought about it far less than in the first few months that followed their engagement.

Ellie's feet moved more swiftly along the pavement the closer she got to the place she called home — the place she'd called home for every one of her twenty-eight years. She'd been away to university and had to share two different flats with friends, but they'd only ever been lodgings. It had always been a relief to return to number twelve, The Copse, where you never had to label your food so that no one else ate it, and nine times out of ten you could smell something delicious baking even before the front door hove into view. Of course the neighbourhood had changed over the years, almost beyond recognition. The small patch of woodland that had once abutted their modest garden and given the road its name — and where Ellie and the neighbours' children had passed hours swinging on an old tyre strung up by one of the dads, or building dens between the closely woven trees — had long been flattened. Now there was a smart new estate shoehorned into the space, with houses that looked out across their own postage-stamp-sized gardens and straight into the garden of number twelve. The patch of woodland and Aunt Hilary's farm had been the two mainstays of her childhood, and they'd seemed almost enchanted back then — only now they were both gone for good.

★   ★   ★

'What's wrong?' Ellie knew immediately that something was. Her mother, Karen, was gripping a piece of good-quality cream paper in one hand, her brow furrowed in the distinctive way that had only meant one thing over the years — official news. In the past, this type of news had always come from solicitors working for her father, detailing why he couldn't meet his financial obligations and, less frequently, asking if he could see Ellie, in the years before she'd turned eighteen and been allowed to answer for herself. Not that her mother had ever stood in her way; she'd always encouraged the visits. But Ellie hadn't failed to notice Karen crossing her fingers when she said that maybe he'd changed this time. He never did, though; he always let Ellie down in the end. Sometimes it was after a week, though more often a month or so would pass with him visiting regularly, but then something better would inevitably come along and he'd disappear again.

Ellie's grandmother would mutter

about her father being a waste of space, her lips disappearing into a thin line of disapproval. Her mother would just smile and squeeze Ellie's hand, saying they were lucky not to have to share her with anyone else. She'd been parent enough for both of them, and Ellie had never really missed her dad. She'd been surrounded by love, strong women, and her gentle grandfather, who was all the male role-model she'd ever needed. Karen had worked all hours, making fancy cakes for weddings, birthdays and every other type of special occasion from their neat little two-up, two-down long before it had been fashionable to start a business making things at home. So Ellie had never had to come back to an empty house, and there was always some marvellous creation on the go, with delicate flowers made from icing that looked so real you could almost smell their scent. When her grandparents had moved to Spain — the warm weather being kinder to her grandfather's asthma — they'd kept an extra-special eye on

Great-aunt Hilary. Not that she'd needed it. She'd been ninety-six, still driving and still living alone at Channel View Farm, right up until the end.

'Mum, did you hear me? What's wrong?' Ellie repeated the question, knowing that this time the official letter couldn't be from her father, who had died years before.

'Oh don't worry, love. Nothing's wrong.' Her mother looked up finally and gave her a wobbly smile. 'Only, I can't get my head around it. Here, you have a look.' She passed Ellie the letter. 'See if I'm reading this all wrong.'

'It says that Aunt Hilary's left the farm to both of us.' Ellie had to pull out one of the pine chairs from the kitchen table and sit down opposite her mother, her legs seeming to have lost the ability to hold her up. Scanning the solicitor's letter again, she shook her head. 'But that can't be right. It was supposed to go to the cats' home. She always said; she always made that perfectly clear.'

'I know. I've been trying to ring

Grandma, to see if she knew anything about Aunt Hilary's intentions — after all, by rights it should go to her; she's always been Hilary's closest sibling — but she never mentioned it when she came over for the funeral.' Karen mirrored her daughter and shook her head. 'It doesn't make any sense.'

'Was there anything else in with the letter?' Ellie took the envelope from her mother and reached inside. There *was* something else in there, and she hoped against hope it would be a letter from her great-aunt; not just because it might explain things, but because it would be like hearing Hilary speak one last time, and that would have been worth more to her than anything. She swallowed her disappointment when she saw that it wasn't a letter, but a leaflet, the really old-fashioned sort that looked like it had been homemade using a typewriter. It was advertising Channel View Farm Donkey Sanctuary. As Ellie began to read the leaflet, with its stuck-on photograph of Gerald III, it blurred in front of her eyes.

'It's one of Aunt Hilary's flyers.' As she started to speak, the phone rang, making both of them jump.

'Sorry, love, I'll have to get that. I just hope it's Grandma and that she can shed some light on all of this.' Her mother disappeared into the other room to take the call, and Ellie turned the leaflet over so that Gerald III's kind old face looked back at her. For a donkey, he'd mastered the sort of regal expression that befitted her great-aunt's favourite. She'd often wondered what had happened to him when Hilary had finally decided to close down the donkey sanctuary two months after her ninetieth birthday. All she'd said was that he'd gone to a loving home; and if the place was good enough for Hilary to send her beloved Gerald to, it was likely to be fit for a king.

The donkey had followed her aunt around like a puppy; everywhere she went on the farm, he went too. Ellie had accompanied Hilary on many a walk down to check the perimeter fence of the farm, where the wooden stakes and surprisingly thin strands of wire were all that stood between the borders of her great-aunt's land, the crumbling cliff face just beyond it, and the English Channel. The farm had never been a 'real' working farm, at least not in Ellie's lifetime. Ten acres of grassland formed a triangle that ran from the cliff face at one edge to the borders of a more traditional arable farm on the other, with a small stretch of road frontage on its remaining side.

Most of the fields were home to the occupants of the donkey sanctuary, who happily shared the space with an assortment of other rescue animals, including sheep, pigs, and several goats. Aunt Hilary had opened the farm to visitors in an attempt to help meet the costs of keeping Gerald and his friends well-fed. It was on one of these trips down to check the fencing that Ellie had finally come to understand why both the farm and the donkeys were so important to her great-aunt. She'd always assumed Hilary had chosen not to marry, preferring the company of her animals, but it wasn't quite as simple as that.

'I never get tired of that view, you know?' Hilary had turned to look at Ellie as they moved along the fence line, pushing against the wooden stakes to ensure they were still secure. Ellie was spending as much of her last summer before university at the farm as she could, knowing that her life was about to change: study would be followed by work, and idyllic weeks at the farm wouldn't be as easy to fit in.

'It's beautiful.' There was a cooling summer breeze, and the wildflowers that dotted the cliff edge just beyond a hungry donkey's reach swayed in unison with the waves washing on the pebbled beach just visible below. White horses danced along the waves, and Ellie could clearly see the cliffs of France across the water. 'Have you ever thought about going somewhere a bit more . . . manageable? If you have to stop driving it will be a really long walk down the hill to the bus stop, and more importantly back up again, just to get into town.'

'Ah, but you're forgetting that I'm Hils by name and hills by nature.' She grinned, suddenly looking at least twenty years younger. 'And as to your question, the answer is no. They'd have to carry me off this cliff kicking and screaming all the time I've breath in my lungs. I'm living the dream that Gerry and I had. I've had to live it for two all these years, so I'm not about to give up just because I'm an octogenarian.'

'Who's Gerry?' Ellie pushed against another of the wooden stakes as she spoke. It was as firmly set into the clay cliff top as if it had been dipped in concrete. There were lots of black-and-white photos dotted around the farmhouse, and as a child she'd been curious about who the people in them were; but the names of long-past relatives had slipped from her memory like grains of sand, so she couldn't be sure if her great-aunt had mentioned Gerry before.

'He was my fiancé.' Hilary smiled again, this time at the look of surprise that Ellie knew must have crossed her face — though it suddenly made sense why her favourite donkeys were always named Gerald. 'We got engaged just before he was called up to war and we planned to get married as soon as he came home. He was going to take over his father's business, giving donkey rides to the tourists on the beaches just around the coast from here where it's sandier and flat. His dad made a good living at Margate; the tourists used to flock in their thousands back then. It would have been too pebbly here, of course. It was a simple enough dream, but we didn't even get that.'

'What happened?' Ellie could guess, but now that Aunt Hilary was finally telling her story, she didn't want her to stop.

'He was killed in the battle of Dunkirk, not far from the French cliffs — you can see across the water. I sometimes stand here and imagine he didn't die at all; that he's just on a cliff top facing me from the other side of the Channel.' Hilary rubbed her eyes with the back of her hand. 'But then, I can be a daft old bat at times.'

'It's not daft at all. It's a lovely way to think about him.' Ellie linked arms with her great-aunt as they walked towards the next row of fencing that needed to be checked. 'And what about the farm? How did you end up here?'

'I never wanted to go out with anyone else after Gerry.' She turned her cornflower-blue eyes towards Ellie, who could see so much written there. 'So I took a job as a housekeeper for the couple who lived here. I thought they were ancient at the time.' She laughed. 'They were probably barely in their fifties, and they were lovely to me; treated me like the daughter they'd never had. I ended up looking after the wife after her husband died, when I'd been working for them for more than twenty years. Ten years after that, Doris went too, and they left all this to me.'

She swept her hands in a circular motion.

'And did you start the donkey rides then?' Hilary had been nearly seventy by the time Ellie was born, so it was perfectly possible she'd had a business giving donkey rides on the beach before that.

'No. That was something I couldn't have done without Gerry, but I could offer the donkeys somewhere to retire.' Hilary pushed against a wooden stake, which barely moved. 'The farm had been wound down over the years, anyway. I had a few sheep and goats, but it wasn't really making enough money to keep going, so I hit on the idea of opening a donkey sanctuary and having a few other animals as well. Petting zoos seemed to be all the rage. I started it just after my fifty-fifth birthday, and here we are thirty years later, still . . . surviving.'

'So is that why you won't retire? Are you worried about who would look after the animals?' Ellie loved the motley collection of donkeys who grazed on the plentiful supply of lush green grass at Channel View, but she knew her great-aunt made do with charity shop hand-me-downs so they'd be well-fed in winter, and she hadn't had a day off from the farm in forever. Petting zoos had given way to roller-coasters over the years, and kids wanted more from a day out than the sanctuary could offer, so making ends meet had become harder and harder.

'I'm under no illusions about what might happen to the place when I'm gone, which is why I'm thinking of leaving it to the cats' home. If there won't be donkeys here, at least it will do some animals a bit of good, and they've always been more loyal than most people I know.' Aunt Hilary had squeezed Ellie's arm as she'd spoken, as if to say that present company was excepted, though she didn't need to say the words out loud. 'No one else would have wanted this life but me and Gerry, and I never wanted anyone else to share it. You only get one life, and I had to live my dreams the best way I could without Gerry in them, but it didn't mean anyone else could take his place. After all, why settle for second best?'

Ellie put the leaflet down, brought back to the present by the sound of her mother opening the kitchen door after finishing her phone call.

'Was that Grandma?' Ellie looked up as her mother nodded. 'Did she know about Aunt Hilary's will?'

'She did.' Karen sat down with a thud and the cake sitting on the dresser behind her jumped ever so slightly to the right. 'Apparently it was always her intention to leave us the farm. She just told everyone it was going to the cats' home to test a theory, to see if the rest of the cousins and their children stopped what she called their duty visits.'

'And they did?' Ellie sighed, not needing an answer.

'Of course. We were her only visitors once Mum and Dad left for Spain.'

'And does she mind? Grandma, I

mean. After all, like you said, she was Hilary's favourite sister.' Ellie felt her stomach turn over at the thought of her grandparents being upset. Without Aunt Hilary to fill the void a little, she missed them more than ever.

'Not a bit. She and Hilary discussed it all, apparently. As she said on the phone, what on earth would they do with a donkey sanctuary?' Karen looked at Ellie, her eyebrows almost disappearing beneath her fringe. 'And what about us? Do we want it?'

'The strange thing is, I think I do.' The words were out of Ellie's mouth before she had a chance to really think it through. 'I've been getting more and more disillusioned with my job, and I hate the commute. Maybe it's what I've been waiting for — a new life in the country and a new job somewhere local to the farm.'

'But what about Rupert? What do you think he'll make of all this?' Her mother grimaced slightly at the prospect.

'I hadn't thought about that.' Ellie

picked up the leaflet for the donkey sanctuary again, her great-aunt's words from ten years earlier ringing in her ears. 'But you only get one life, and Rupert will be happy as long as I am.' Crossing her fingers under the table for luck, she added, 'I'm sure he will.'

2

Ellie was feeling much less sure about anything by the time they pulled up into the yard of Channel View Farm. It had been years since they'd been up to the farm itself. Aunt Hilary had insisted on meeting them in town once she'd shut the sanctuary and rehomed the animals. She'd said it had given her a reason to get out and about, as there were far too few of those. But now that Ellie was out of the car and looking around at the state of the place, she couldn't help but think her great-aunt had been driven by an ulterior motive for keeping them away.

'I can't believe it's the same place.' She jumped as an ear-splitting hee-haw cut across the yard and literally rattled the wooden window frames of the farmhouse, which itself had seen far better days.

'I should have known better when Hilary insisted on meeting us in town.' Karen shot Ellie a look of alarm as the hee-hawing reached a crescendo.

'And if that's not Gerald, who she told me had been rehomed years ago, then I'll eat the straw hat he used to wear giving donkey rides.' Ellie led the way around the back of the farmhouse and down the shingle path toward the largest of the paddocks, where a moth-eaten-looking Gerald was staring mournfully over a fence that didn't look like it would have held up if the donkey had given it a good push.

'Oh God, do you think anyone's been looking after him since the funeral?' All the colour had drained out of Karen's face and Ellie's throat tightened at the thought of her aunt's beloved donkey being half-starved without her to care for him. Though if anything, Gerald looked a bit on the hefty side.

'There's a bucket of grain in the corner, so someone's been looking after him.' The words were hardly out of

Karen's mouth before a deep voice behind them made them both jump again.

'Someone's been looking after him, all right. And the rest of the menagerie. And someone still is. The question is, who the hell are you?'

Ellie took in the man's appearance. He was probably in his late fifties, wearing wellies that looked like they'd seen better days and an expression bordering on contempt.

'We might ask you the same question, since it's you who's trespassing on our land.' Her mother was bristling as she spoke, and Ellie placed a hand on her arm.

'Sorry, you just took us by surprise, that's all.' Ellie held out her other hand and tried not to notice how filthy the mystery man's rough red hands looked. 'This is my mother, Karen Chapman — Hilary's niece, and I'm Ellie.' She might have been insulted that Mr Angry ignored her outstretched hand, but she couldn't help feeling a little bit relieved.

'Oh, I see. The vultures are closing in now, are they? No one's been near or by for years, but you're here now there are goods and chattel to price up. Typical of your generation.' Disgust was written all over his face.

'Not that it's any of your business, Mr — ?' Karen paused and eventually the man grumbled his name. 'Not that it's any of your business, Mr Crabtree, but I met with my aunt at least once a week and I always asked to meet her here. Since she shut the sanctuary, though, she always wanted to meet me in town.'

'Any half-wit could have worked out the reason for that.' Mr Crabtree was not going to be easily thawed, and Ellie wondered for the first time if it wouldn't just be easier to sell the farm and walk away. 'Your aunt was a proud woman; she wouldn't want to ask for help. It nearly killed her to take it off me, and we'd been friends and neighbours my whole life. Not that I had the time or money to help her properly. The place has gone to ruin, but I suppose you'll sell it now to some God-awful weekenders from London who just want somewhere for their spoilt kids to roar around on their quad bikes. Then what will happen to Gerald and the others? Dog food, I'll bet.'

'Look, I'm sorry we've got off on the wrong foot,' Ellie interjected before her mother could speak. Karen's cheeks were turning red and it looked like she was on the edge of tears. 'But we've got no intention of selling to weekenders, or any-one for that matter.' If she'd been wavering, another glance at Gerald's mournful face was enough to convince her. Added to which, she wasn't about to prove Mr Crabtree right if she could help it.

'Hmm, I'll believe it when I see it.' Mr Crabtree shrugged his shoulders as if he couldn't care less, but his face told an entirely different story. 'When you've finished working out how much money you can wring out of the farm, you might want to get Gerald looked at by a vet. Animals aren't my forte and I could only do my best. He's been lame these last couple of days and I've been meaning to call Ben, but like I said I'm not made of money.' With another shrug, he disappeared back up the track, and Ellie let out a long breath.

'He was charming,' she muttered. 'But what I don't understand is, if he was such a good friend of Aunt Hilary's, how come we never met him in all the years we were coming to the farm?'

'He strikes me as someone who keeps himself to himself.' The colour in Karen's cheeks was gradually returning to normal. 'I think I might have met his parents in the past, but I think I remember Hilary telling me that the son was a bit awkward when he was a lad. Seems to have got more so over the years, rather than growing out of it.'

'Well, the more he keeps himself to himself the better, as far as I'm concerned.' Ellie shivered at the thought of encountering their grumpy new neighbour again. It was almost worse than the thought of breaking the news of their planned move to Rupert. 'Come on, let's go and see how bad the house is inside, and I'll try and track down that vet's number. If the sound Gerald is making is any indication of how much pain he's in, the vet better get here quick.'

*　*　*

The house was just as Ellie had feared it might be when she'd seen the state of repair of the rest of the farm. The kitchen, the front room, her great-aunt's old bedroom, and the upstairs bathroom weren't too bad. She'd obviously kept on top of the areas she used the most. Hilary had never been one to spend much on herself, and that included the furniture. Nothing matched, and her bedspread had been patched more than a dozen times, though at least those rooms were fairly clean and things had been repaired. There was dust from a lack of use over the past few weeks, but they were liveable — just about. At some point her aunt had obviously started closing up the other rooms, which had locks built into the old-fashioned heavy oak doors. Ellie found a set of keys in the kitchen, each one with a luggage label attached in her great-aunt's loopy writing. Some rooms were bare, but the peeling wallpaper and windows — which had begun to leak over the years — left a distinctive scent of neglect. Other rooms were stuffed with bric-a-brac and furniture, everything from broken vases to a stool with two of its three legs missing. They'd expected to have to do a bit of work to make the house habitable, but this was a different prospect entirely.

'Is he here already?' Ellie asked, coming back into the kitchen after opening up the last of the rooms. She'd found the number for the vet on the noticeboard above the kitchen table when they'd first gone into the farmhouse, and he was due to arrive in ten minutes. Her mother was peering out of the window and crossing her fingers that it *was* the vet, rather than the unwelcome return of Mr Crabtree.

'Not yet.' Karen turned away from the window to face her daughter. 'I was just looking out at the yard, thinking how much there is to put right. Do you think we're biting off more than we can chew?' She had been busy scrubbing the kitchen while Ellie checked out the rest of the house. Ellie was wearing one of Aunt Hilary's pinnies, and it already looked like a different place — somewhere she could imagine her mum baking delicious cakes and having the life she'd more than earned over the years. If Ellie had to make some sacrifices to make that happen, it was only a bit of payback for everything that Karen had done for her over the years.

'It'll be fine, especially if Joan's sister wants to buy our old place. We can use the money to put things right here.' Ellie put an arm around her mother's waist. 'We'll make Aunt Hilary proud.'

'Joan was almost certain that Ruby would move in like a shot.' For the first time since meeting Mr Crabtree, there was a hint of a smile on Karen's face.

Their neighbour's sister was a regular visitor and the two women were close, but Joan had confided that she couldn't live with her full-time. They'd asked if Ruby could have first refusal if Karen ever decided to sell the house, so a ready-made buyer for the old place looked like it could well be on the cards. Karen smiled again as another of Gerald's ear-splitting hee-haws crossed the yard. 'And we could give Gerald the retirement he deserves.'

'Talking of which, it looks like the vet's arrived.' The sound of tyres on gravel was a welcome reassurance that help was at hand. 'We'll get the old boy and this place sorted out, Mum. It'll be all right, it really will.' Ellie returned her mum's smile and pushed down the thought she'd been trying to supress for days. Rupert would be back from his business trip on Monday, and she couldn't put off the news any longer. For all her bravado that he'd be happy for her and that everything would be okay, she couldn't quite convince herself that her fiancé would see things in the same light.

★   ★   ★

'I've got a good mind to report you to the RSPCA.' Ben Hastings shot Ellie a look that made Mr Crabtree's introduction from earlier look positively welcoming. 'This donkey's got laminitis. He's been gorging himself on all the spring grass he's got access to because your paddocks aren't properly fenced, and he's got all this grain here too.' He jabbed a finger towards the bucket.

'I was worried he might be too thin.' Ellie bit her lip. It hadn't been the easiest of days, and she already felt terrible that Gerald and the few remaining animals at the farm were in such a bad state.

'Can't you see this?' Ben pointed to the donkey's pendulous belly, his dark eyes fixing on her face, giving her nowhere to hide. She'd been determined not to cry and had held it all together in the face of Mr Crabtree's wrath, but she knew Ben was only angry because he cared so much about animals. He'd been perfectly friendly until he'd set eyes on Gerald.

'I've only been here three hours!' Ellie's voice went at least an octave higher and she dug her nails into her hand, trying to stop the tears that were still threatening. 'It's the miserable old man from next door you want to take this up with.' She'd had enough of being pushed around and criticised for one day.

'Alan Crabtree?' Ben ran a hand through his black hair, and this time when he looked at her there was far less narrowing of the eyes. 'He's a bit of a tartar, isn't he?'

'That's one word for him.' Ellie could have sworn she saw a hint of a smile twitching at the corners of his mouth.

'I'm sorry, I should have found out more about what's been going on before I had a go at you. I just hate seeing animals end up like this.' Ben patted the old donkey on his rump and a cloud of dust rose up from Gerald's coat, making them both cough. 'You've got your work cut out getting the animals back to their best, never mind the rest of the place. What's the plan for the farm?'

'My great-aunt left it to us, but she hadn't let us visit her here for several years. Now we know why. She told us she'd got rid of all the animals, but I think she was scared that if she sent them somewhere else, they might end up . . . ' Ellie felt the desire to cry for an entirely different reason as Gerald began nuzzling her pocket, reminding her of the way Hilary had always kept some pony nuts in her pocket for her best boy. She'd be horrified to see him like this.

'Well, if you're going to sell up, the kindest thing to do might be just that — to let the old boy go.' Though Ben said the words, he didn't sound very convinced, and there was no way Ellie would let that happen.

'Absolutely not!' The donkey was still

nuzzling at her pocket. If she was going to have to put him on a diet, it wasn't going to be easy. 'We're not selling, and we're not going to let anything happen to Gerald either. There must be something you can do for him.'

'The first step would be an anti-inflammatory injection. Then you'll have to treat him with painkillers and hose his legs down every few hours.' Ben was already opening his leather treatment bag. 'After that, you'll have to get the farrier out to do some remedial work on his feet, and I'd suggest keeping him in a stable with a deep bed of wood shavings. I also think he'd benefit from having a relief boot on his front right hoof.'

'That sounds doable.' It was Ellie's turn to sound less than convinced. This was all Greek to her.

'It won't be cheap, and it's a lot of work.' He unwrapped the syringe he'd taken from the case.

'He's worth it.' Ellie watched as Ben loaded the syringe with anti-inflammatory medication. The donkey barely even seemed to notice the needle going in, the poor old thing already being in so much pain.

'I'll have to come up and see him every couple of days to make sure the treatment's working,' Ben said. He took a long plastic tube of painkilling paste out of his bag and handed it to Ellie. 'You'll need to limit his food to a pad of hay a day. You'll also need to syringe a dose of the painkiller into the corner of his mouth, and keep up the hosing. Do you need me to write it down for you?' He looked up at her, and this time the smile moved more than the corners of his mouth. He had even white teeth and a deep dimple in his right cheek when he smiled properly. Suddenly the thought of seeing him every couple of days was strangely cheering.

'I think I'll be all right, but is it okay to call you if I'm worried about him?' Ellie felt pure relief as he nodded. Maybe the locals wouldn't be entirely hostile after all.

3

'I thought you'd be waiting at the flat for me when I got back.' The tone of Rupert's voice was somewhere between husky and sulky, probably closer to the latter. Ellie couldn't really blame him — she'd always been at his beck and call before. That was the way it went when you were with someone you felt was way out of your league and they did absolutely nothing to reassure you otherwise.

'I've been busy. A few unexpected thing came up.' She didn't elaborate. This wasn't a conversation she wanted to have over the phone, and Rupert clearly wasn't interested enough to ask. Maybe it was just dread at how he might react, but she felt like she was slipping out of the spell Rupert had held her under for far too long. Had he always been like this — only interested in himself?

'So when are you coming up then?'
He paused for a moment, and when she
didn't immediately answer he added as
an afterthought, 'I missed you.'

'That's nice.' She wanted to ask him
if he meant it, and what it was exactly
he'd missed about her. She knew she
should probably reciprocate and tell
him she'd missed him too, but she
didn't do that either. The truth was, she
wasn't sure she had. She told herself it
was just because she'd been so busy
and so much had changed while he'd
been away. It was Sunday night, she was
back in the old house, and her mother
had gone next door to speak to Ruby
and Joan about buying the house. From
her one-sided eavesdropping of the call
earlier, it seemed like more or less a
done deal. She had the Sunday-night
blues and work was beckoning — a
well-paid but unfulfilling job in events
management for a city bank that sadly
she couldn't afford to just quit. It was
how she'd met Rupert, at one of their
corporate hospitality events at Ascot.

She'd enjoyed the job once upon a time, but for the last few months it had increasingly lost its sheen. The commute was stifling, and most of the people she met at work weren't the sort she'd have chosen to spend her time with. Her every waking thought was now filled with the farm, and even the prospects of bumping into Alan Crabtree or getting another telling-off from Ben the vet were preferable to facing a week in the office and the commuting that went with it.

'I got you a little something whilst I was away, to let you know just how much I was thinking of you.' Rupert had a bit of a track record for buying her what you might call self-improvement presents — everything from lip-plumping solutions to a book about the seven habits of highly successful people. So she wasn't exactly gripped with excitement at the thought of his latest gift. 'Will you come over after work tomorrow? I should be done by seven.'

'I'll be there. Love you.' She said the

words automatically, but they felt different than they had a week before. Was Aunt Hilary's bequest about to change far more than just her postcode?

⋆　⋆　⋆

Her mother was smiling as she came back through the front door, but Ellie still held her breath. This could be it — their chance to move to the farm almost straight away. Yes, it would make the commute worse than ever, but the thought of what she'd be coming home to each night made Ellie smile.

Karen was going back to the farm in the morning. They'd paid one of the veterinary nurses to go up and bathe Gerald's legs in their absence, but just a night of one-to-one donkey nursing was costing a small fortune — Karen had to bake a lot of cakes to earn that sort of money, and it wasn't something they could sustain for long. Ellie tried not to ponder the financial side of things too much; when she thought about the farm she preferred the romantic to the practical. It would all work out one way or another. Her mother could expand the business once they'd updated the kitchen and she'd established herself; maybe even get her cakes into some of the local shops. Ellie would get a job closer to the farm at some point. It would be okay. This was the mantra she repeated to herself when she woke up at night in a panic, and she was sticking to it.

'How did it go?' Ellie asked her mother. She had been staring at her laptop on the pretext of looking at jobs close to the farm, but she couldn't concentrate, straining to try and hear something through the thick walls that separated the house from next door. Anything that might give her an indication of whether Ruby still wanted the house.

'Put it this way — it's worthy of the last couple of slices of cake and two big cups of tea.'

Karen smiled again. 'Only we'd

better wash up straight away, because if Ruby gets things her way she'll be moving in before the teapot's cold!'

'Really?' Ellie leapt up and allowed herself to be folded into her mother's arms. It was still just as comforting as it had been in her childhood. 'Can you believe we're really going to do this?'

'It's starting to feel a bit more real.' Karen moved toward the kettle as Ellie pulled away. Her mum was like lightening in the kitchen. Within seconds a tray had been beautifully laid with everything required for the perfect cup of tea. The flowered teapot sat next to matching cups and saucers, and a bowl with uneven brown and white lumps of sugar and a pair of antique silver tongs.

Karen spun round, a look of panic suddenly crossing her face. 'You're not regretting the decision or worrying about what Rupert's going to say, are you?'

'No. Well, that's not strictly true. I have been thinking about what Rupert will say, but I'm not having second thoughts.' Ellie squeezed her mum's arm. 'It's the chance of a lifetime, the way I see it. And if Rupert doesn't think so, well . . . ' She hesitated, unsure how to finish the sentence.

'Is everything okay with you two?' Karen loaded the tea tray with two more tea-plates, this time laden with generous slices of lighter-than-air Victoria sponge.

'Yes . . . I think so . . . I don't know.' Ellie shrugged. 'I'm sure it's just him being so busy at work, and loving it so much, and me feeling so flat about my job. We just seem to be moving in different directions these days. But I'm sure the farm will give me back my oomph and things will go back to being like they used to be with Rupert.'

'I just don't want you to feel like you've got to do this because of me.' Karen poured boiling water onto the teabags.

'I'm not, I promise. I can't get what Hilary said out of my head, when she first told me about the original Gerald — life shouldn't be about settling for second best. That's what my job is now.

But life at the farm, maybe that really could be the dream.' She opened the door that led to the lounge and took the tea tray off her mum to carry through. It was her job that was second best, not Rupert. He was a catch, after all; everyone said so. She was sure once her move to the farm was sorted and she changed her job, their relationship would be back on track too . . . well, almost sure.

* * *

'Ah, Ellie, just the person.' Will Naysmith was the director of corporate services at the bank where she worked, which made him her boss. 'Can I see you in my office?' It was a command rather than a request, and she nodded, silently racking her brain for what she might have done wrong.

'Take a seat, and don't look so worried.' He smiled frequently, but it never quite reached his eyes — which were shark-like, as though he was always on the lookout for the next opportunity. His office was a status symbol, all dark furniture with black leather and shiny chrome chairs; and Ellie's chair was much lower than his so that she was at an immediate disadvantage. 'How was your annual leave?' He asked the question, but she knew he wasn't really interested, so she just nodded and returned his smile. 'Good, good. I hope you got some rest, because things are about to get interesting.'

'Oh?' Ellie very much doubted that. The things that Will and his ilk in the banking world found interesting had never really done much for her, and now less than ever. It was bound to be some big launch event for a new type of current account, or an interest-rate-tracking mortgage. Ellie fought the urge to yawn.

'The bank has decided to move in a different direction with its events. Contracting out the service to an events management company will ultimately save money and make use of even more specialised services.' The smile was still plastered on Will's face, even as he was telling her she was about to lose her job.

'Right, so they won't need my role anymore?' She must have looked as shocked as she felt, and Will laid a hand on her arm.

'Well, that's true. But the good news is that Uncle Will has sorted it all for you.' The grip on her arm got stronger, but she was confused.

'Sorry, I'm not quite sure I'm following.'

'That's why I'm the boss.' This time he winked. 'The bank has contracted one of the top events management firms in London, Gerald Hilary and Co., but I told them all about you. What an asset you've been.' He leant forward, as though expecting her to return the compliment. 'So they've agreed to take you on as part of the contract. You'll be working for them, but stay based here *with me*. A lot better than redundancy, don't you think?' He gave her a look that suggested the answer was obvious, but it was like seeing a chink of light at the end of a long, dark tunnel.

'So redundancy's an option?' She could hear her heartbeat whooshing in her ears, terrified that her escape route might be taken away as quickly as it had appeared. She'd always been good at maths, and a quick calculation in her head told her that redundancy from the bank after nearly ten years of service would provide a sizeable nest egg to help get things straight at the farm.

'Well, yes, but of course I told them you wouldn't want that; wouldn't want to stop working here . . . with me,' he emphasised that particular benefit again. 'And Gerald Hilary is a very prestigious firm.'

Somehow the name hadn't quite registered the first time round, but when it did she couldn't stop the smile from slowly spreading across her face. It was obviously meant to be: a firm sharing the name of her great-aunt and her lost fiancé was giving Ellie the chance to escape from the job she hated. It was almost as if Hilary was sending her a message.

'Actually, I think taking the redundancy might be best all round.' She was already getting up from her seat and heading towards where Will's PA sat, just outside the glass wall of his office, before Will had the chance to somehow take away the option. 'I'll get Janey to give HR a call and sort out the details, but I know the bank's policy on redundancy. I can have my desk cleared by lunchtime.' With shaking legs, Ellie pushed open the office door, taking the first steps towards her newfound freedom.

* * *

Rupert's apartment was in a converted warehouse overlooking the Thames. He worked hard and had all the material things to prove it, from his beloved red sports car to the bachelor pad that Ellie had always known she could never call home. It was loft-style, airy and open-plan, with little more than an assortment of high-tech gadgets and large sofas to sully its perfect simplicity. There were no family photographs, ornaments or holiday souvenirs to clutter it up; it was the very opposite of Aunt Hilary's place or even the house in The Copse, where her mother had covered every inch of shelf space with photographs and mementos of their family life. If felt cold in Rupert's flat, which had nothing to do with the temperature.

'I've missed you.' Rupert repeated his words of the night before as he kissed her, and she desperately wanted to feel the frisson of excitement that had always come so easily in the past, but it wasn't there. It was nerves, that was all — telling him about the farm and the redundancy was going to be a lot for him to take in, and now that she was here she was less convinced than ever that he would see how good it could be for her . . . for them.

'You too,' she said. It wasn't strictly true; but she had thought about him, and how he'd react, a lot. 'How was your business trip?' As director of acquisitions for a large property development company, Rupert was away more often than he was at home. Ellie had always envied him his job, and he'd acquired some wonderful properties over the years she'd known him. She'd always loved the period properties, but Rupert preferred the new builds, or period places like his own that had been given a thoroughly modern makeover. He'd absolutely hate the farm, and the realisation made her shiver.

'It was good,' he replied. 'We bought an old chateau. It needs gutting, of course.' Rupert was already pouring her a drink, choosing what she'd have without even asking. She could just imagine his view of a chateau filled with original features — depressing and outdated was usually the way he described old things. A dilapidated Grade 2 listed farmhouse deep in the Kent countryside was unlikely to illicit much warmth. 'It's going to be a luxury wedding venue when it's finished, though. All that's big business these days.'

'Sounds lovely.' She meant it. Organising weddings was a million times closer to what she'd hoped she'd be doing when she'd studied for her events management degree, instead of organising cocktail parties for over-privileged bankers.

'That reminds me, I've got that present for you.' Rupert handed her a glass of red wine which was no doubt good quality but tasted like metal in her mouth. He disappeared into his bedroom for a moment before re-emerging with a large brown bag with rope handles.

'Saucepans?' Ellie looked from the Le Creuset pans in the bag up to Rupert and back down again.

'Only the best for you, my darling.' He looked absolutely delighted with his gift, and she did her best to return his smile. 'After all, I think it's about time that you extended your repertoire from bacon sandwiches and pot noodles to something a bit more suitable for my wife-to-be. We'll have to do a lot of entertaining once we're married, and these will help you get some practice in.'

'Bacon sandwiches will taste all the better made in these.' She wanted to laugh and ask him if he was joking, but she knew he wasn't. If she'd been hesitant in telling him about the farm, now felt like as good a time as any. 'They'll actually be great in the farm-house, and Mum will love them.'

'Farmhouse?' Rupert's voice had already taken on an edge of suspicion, but she had no choice but to plough on.

'Turns out Aunt Hilary left the farm to Mum and me.' She didn't pause for breath; it was too risky to give him a chance to interrupt. 'And our neigh-bour's sister has agreed to buy our house. She's got cash and wants to move in as soon as possible, so there's nothing stopping us going for it.'

'Nothing?' He arched an eyebrow.

'What about your job? What about me?'

'I was made redundant today.' She wouldn't tell him it was her choice; that was an explanation for her mum's ears only. 'And I thought you'd be pleased. It's a great place, and we always agreed we wouldn't move in together until after the wedding. I couldn't live here, you know that; and being away so much, you could base yourself anywhere.'

'Are you seriously expecting me to move to a farmhouse in the middle of nowhere with you . . . and your mum?' Rupert looked incredulous.

'I suppose I didn't think it would matter to you if Mum was there or not.'

'No, you didn't think. That much is clear.' He drained his glass in one and set it down on the table. His reaction wasn't entirely unexpected, but she'd wanted him to surprise her. If he'd said that being with her was the important thing and it didn't matter where, the doubts she'd had about their relationship would have dissolved. As it was, the thought of heading home — to her mum and the farm — was more appealing than ever.

4

'Can you just run me through every-thing on the list again, so we can sort out the absolute essentials first?' The number on the calculator couldn't be right. Ellie shook her head, hoping that it might change the figure on the digital display. The stack of estimates on the kitchen table, the cost of putting things right at the farm, didn't make for pretty reading either.

'The surveyor said we need new win-dows, and because it's a listed cottage they've got to be handmade wooden case-ments.' Karen sighed, still beating the cake mix as though her life depended on it. 'Then the roof needs replacing — which can only be with Kent peg tiles. The electrics are apparently a museum piece, and potentially lethal to boot. And I'm sure you've noticed that the plumbing makes rattling noises like Marley's chains as soon as you turn a tap on. I'm afraid if we want to make it to the end of our first year alive, the repairs are all pretty much essential.'

'Just a few little tweaks, then.' Ellie tried to smile, but she could see her redundancy money and the profits from the old house disappearing faster than you could say money pit. 'And what about the outside? Do you think there's anything that desperately needs doing out there?'

'Well, the good news is that the stables and most of the outbuildings, including the old barn, seem to be holding up okay.' Karen spooned the mixture into cake papers as she spoke. 'But the bad news is that almost all of the fencing needs to be replaced; and the absolute worst part of that is that one of us will have to go and see Alan Crabtree to check which parts of the fencing belong to him and which belong to us. I can only imagine what sort of reaction it will provoke if we get that wrong!'

'That *is* bad news.' Ellie laughed at the expression on her mum's face. 'So what's the plan of attack?'

'What do you think I'm making these fairy cakes for?' Karen raised an eyebrow. 'They're intended as a peace offering, though if all else fails I can always throw them at him!'

'It's always worth having a backup plan where Alan Crabtree's concerned.' Ellie scanned down the list of things that needed to be paid for again. 'We can't forget the vet bills, of course. I think we should get all the animals checked over now that Gerald seems to be on the mend.'

'You wouldn't have an ulterior motive at all, would you, my love?' Karen winked and a blush swept across Ellie's face. Of course she genuinely wanted the best for the animals in their care — Aunt Hilary had entrusted them with her most treasured possessions — but she was finding it hard to deny that seeing Ben again wasn't an added bonus. He'd been a regular visitor since that first night when he'd given her such a hard time. Despite such an unpromising start, he was proving to be one of the nicest things about moving to Kelsea Bay, the small town which Aunt Hilary's farm perched on the edge of.

'Just because I'm single, it doesn't mean I'm desperate to find someone new,' she told her mum. 'Promise me you won't drop any heavy hints when Ben's around. The last thing I want is another relationship so soon, even if he is as nice as he looks.' Ellie's face grew hotter still as she said the words out loud; suddenly the pile of estimates in front of her seemed really interesting. She was in danger of acting like a schoolgirl when it came to Ben Hastings.

'So it's definite, then — you and Rupert are finished for good.' Her mum didn't sound at all upset at the prospect, but then Ellie knew she'd never really warmed to him. Ben, on the other hand, was a different matter. Every time he arrived at the farm, Karen would announce that the kettle was on, and she never failed to have a large slice of his favourite gypsy tart waiting for him.

'I think Rupert made it pretty clear we were at an impasse the last time we spoke, the day after I told him about inheriting this place,' Ellie said. 'He didn't even wait to see me again, so we could talk it through; he just rang and said he'd thought about it overnight and it was him or the farm. Here I am, a farm girl all the way, and it isn't like he's pulled out all the stops to try and win me back.' She grinned. It didn't even hurt to talk about Rupert anymore. She'd been surprised by how easy the choice was when it finally came down to it. 'I suppose it won't be a hundred percent official until I've returned the ring. But next time I get the opportunity to see him face to face, I'll be doing that too.' She glanced at the fourth finger of her left hand, where the white gold and diamond band had left a line of slightly paler skin. After a summer at the farm that would disappear too, and the last physical reminder of her relationship with Rupert would disappear with it.

* * *

Gerald's head appeared above the stable door as soon as he heard someone crossing the yard outside. The old donkey appeared to be almost smiling at Ellie and Ben, a piece of hay sticking out between his big yellow teeth.

'You've done a great job with him, you know.' Ben, who'd come to give him another check-over, ran a hand down the donkey's leg. 'I think he's ready to go back outside. Have you fenced off a starvation paddock?'

'We have.' Ellie nodded. 'Although I still can't get used to that expression. It sounds so cruel.'

'Far crueller to let him get laminitis again.' Ben looked up at her, his warm brown eyes crinkling in the corners. All of the animosity from their first meeting had long since melted away. 'You should be proud of yourself. I honestly didn't think we could save him, what with his age and everything. But you've worked miracles, bathing his legs every few hours and resisting those puppy-dog eyes of his begging you for just a bit more food.'

'It's true, he can give you a look that's pretty hard to resist!' Running a hand through her hair, Ellie fought the urge to add that the donkey wasn't alone in having that effect on her. She'd told her mum not to drop any heavy hints, but Karen wasn't the only one in danger of giving the game away.

'I've been meaning to ask you some-thing, only I wasn't quite sure how to say it.' Ben didn't look at her again as he spoke. Instead he made a great show of checking over the donkey's other legs. 'I . . . wondered what had happened to your engagement ring. I noticed it the first time we met, but you haven't been wearing it lately, and — '

'It's because I'm not engaged anymore.'

Ellie patted the donkey's neck. 'He didn't like the idea of life on a farm.'

'I'm sorry.'

'I'm not.' Ellie smiled. 'I'd started to realise I didn't like the idea of life with him much, on a farm or anywhere else for that matter. But it was only inheriting this place that made it all crystal clear.'

'In that case, I'm not sorry either.' Ben straightened up and returned her smile, the dimple deepening in his right cheek. 'In fact I'm really glad you're single, because it makes it all the easier to ask you another question. There's a barn dance in the church hall on Saturday and I'm expected to go. I wondered if you might like to come with me, to meet some of the other locals. It's usually a good night, and they do a fantastic hog roast.'

'You had me at 'barn dance'.' Ellie laughed, her earlier vow to steer clear of anything new happily forgotten. 'You might think I'm a city girl, but believe me, I can do-si-do with the best of them.'

'It's a date, then?' He raised a questioning eyebrow.

'I do believe it is, Mr Hastings. And I just hope your square dancing doesn't let you down!'

★　★　★

Balancing a cake box on one arm whilst trying to climb over a rickety wooden stile wasn't the easiest of things to do. Karen was sure that Alan Crabtree had seen her crossing the boundary to his land, but he hadn't rushed to relieve her of her load or even called out to see if she wanted any help. She wasn't about to ask him for help either, or give him another excuse to start ranting about something she'd done wrong; at least this way she'd have a chance to explain the reason for her visit. He was tinkering under the bonnet of a tractor, which looked like it had seen better days decades before.

'Whatever it is you're selling, I'm not interested.' Alan didn't look up, leaving

Karen in no doubt that he'd ignored her struggle over the stile on purpose.

'I'm not selling anything. I brought you this as a gift.' She put the box of fairy cakes on the tractor's step. If she'd been waiting for a thank-you, it would be a long time coming.

'Experience has taught me there's no such thing as a free lunch.' At last he looked up from the rusty engine and caught Karen's eye. 'So what do you want?'

'I don't want anything. I needed to ask you something, though.'

'Want, need — it's all the same thing, just dressed up a different way.' Alan didn't move to look in the box, and Karen was more desperate than ever to get back to the farm and away from their crotchety neighbour.

'We're getting the fencing replaced and we wanted to know which of the boundaries belonged to you and which to us, so that we didn't take down any fencing that's yours.' She glanced around at the ramshackle state of Crabtree Farm, which if anything looked to be in a worse state of repair than their own place.

'It's perfectly simple. The fence on the left-hand side of your land is assigned to you. It's all in the deeds.' He sounded as though she'd asked him the same question a hundred times before. 'But since the boundary on the right follows the cliff top, you'll pretty much have to replace the whole thing.' If he had any sympathy for what that might cost them, he was doing a pretty good job of hiding it.

'Okay, well that sounds simple enough. We'll be getting someone in to replace it. There'll be some other building work going on at the farmhouse too. I hope it won't disturb you.' Karen waited for a moment in the vain hope that Alan might say something to indicate he was pleased by this news, happy to see the farm being taken care of at last. But all he did was grunt and continue poking around under the tractor's hood. So much for the friendliness of neighbours in small communities. Alan Crabtree had as much social grace as one of the potatoes he farmed, and was about as much fun to talk to.

* * *

'How did your peace mission with Alan go?' Ellie asked as she came into the kitchen, which had been one of the first rooms to receive a makeover. They'd chosen a soft baby-blue shade for the walls and given the cupboards a new lease of life by painting them butter-cream. Whilst a new kitchen would have been lovely, it wasn't high up on their ever-growing list of priorities. It looked like home, though, all the same. The shelves of the dresser were crammed with Karen's recipe books; and the ornaments, which had covered every surface at the old house, had found new homes dotted around the kitchen and downstairs rooms. They'd kept the things that were precious to Aunt Hilary, too, and pride of place on the mantelpiece had gone to a black-and-white photograph of her and the original

Gerald on the day they'd got engaged.

'The conversation with Alan went pretty much how you might expect.' Karen smiled as she lined some baking trays with greaseproof paper, seemingly unfazed by her encounter with the neighbour from hell. They'd both accepted that life at the farm might be a bit isolated. It was never going to be like it had been with their neighbours back at The Copse — Karen going next door for games of cards or Scrabble, and fish-and-chip suppers, on Friday evenings when Ellie had been out with Rupert. From time to time she'd worried that her mother didn't have a social life with people more her own age, but she'd always seemed happy — baking, looking in on the neighbours, and generally running around after Ellie. Karen's life had revolved around being a mum for so long that it didn't take a genius to work out she'd sidelined her own needs over the years. But this was a fresh start for them both, and it was a long time since Ellie had needed looking after in that way. Perhaps Alan wasn't the best candidate to start building a new social life with, but Kelsea Bay was a small community and there were plenty of opportunities to make friends. Maybe she could persuade her mum to join her and Ben at the barn dance for a start.

'I take it that by going as expected, you mean that Alan completely ignored you.' Ellie flicked idly through the local paper as she spoke. It had been delivered whilst she was out at the paddock with Ben, but looking for a job in Kelsea Bay was proving more difficult than she'd expected. The only local vacancies had been in some of the shops in town, and even that was mostly seasonal work during the late spring and summer months when the tourists were drawn to pretty coastal towns like theirs. She was determined not to panic and rush into the wrong job, but as the weeks slipped past from April into May, it was getting more pressing to find something — and soon.

'He didn't completely ignore me. He grunted something, insulted me a bit, and *then* ignored me!' Karen laughed, and the baking tray she was holding slipped out of her hands as Gerald III gave one of his ear-splitting hee-haws. 'Goodness, he's got a healthy pair of lungs on him. I don't think I'll ever get used to the sound he makes. I jump out of my skin every time!' As Gerald's braying died down, it was replaced by what sounded like someone running across the gravel outside. Ellie moved over to the window, but there was no one in sight.

'Did you hear that?' She turned to Karen, who shook her head. 'I'm sure there was someone outside. I'd better take a look, in case it's someone from the fencing company wanting to start measuring up. The foreman did say he'd try and get someone up here this afternoon.'

Pulling back the heavy front door of the farmhouse, Ellie immediately saw the old pottery bottle sitting in the middle of the large stone slabs that flanked the doorstep. There were five or six foxglove stems poked inside and a folded piece of paper tucked underneath. Picking it all up, she went back through to the kitchen.

'Where on earth did they come from? They're beautiful — such vibrant colours! And that bottle looks like an antique.' Karen took the bottle from her daughter and set it down on the windowsill, where it looked as though it had always belonged. It fitted the farmhouse perfectly. The foxgloves had rows of flowers in shades of pink, cream and lilac, each one like a little bell. 'They're lovely, and I'm guessing they're from Ben?'

Ellie opened the folded piece of paper, expecting her mum to be right. There was a warm feeling in her stomach at the thought. She read the letter out loud:

Dear Mrs Chapman,
    Thank you for the fairy cakes. They brought back memories and were almost

as good as my mother used to make.
Regards,
Alan Crabtree
P.S. Do let me know if you need a hand with the fencing when the time comes.

He had surprisingly nice writing for someone whose hands looked like they hadn't held a pen in years. Karen's cheeks had coloured slightly at hearing the contents of the letter.

'It's a *sort* of compliment, I suppose.' She was clearly attempting to shrug it off. 'My cakes are *almost* as good as his mother used to make!'

'I wonder why he didn't knock?' Ellie met her mother's eyes for the briefest of moments as she spoke; they both knew the answer. For whatever reason, Alan Crabtree found it very difficult to be friendly — in person, at least — but it seemed he was trying to offer an olive branch in the guise of the five foxglove stems.

'It's very kind of him.' Karen didn't

sound entirely convinced. 'But I won't be rushing back to his farm the moment the flowers die off, hoping for a repeat performance. I'm not sure I can cope with more than one encounter with Alan in a week.'

'I think that's as much as anyone can be expected to do!' Ellie laughed again at the look on her mother's face. It would take more than the delivery of some hand-picked flowers to convince either of them that Alan had changed his spots.

'What about you?' Karen asked her. 'How did it go with Ben? I forgot to ask you what the verdict on Gerald was.'

'He's fighting fit.' Ellie glanced at the flyer her mother had pinned to the noticeboard. 'In fact, if he carries on like this, he might even be well enough to make a brief return from retirement at the summer fundraiser.' The leaflet was advertising Kelsea Bay's twice-yearly event where all sorts of stall-holders set up shop for a single day to raise funds for the church hall and the mayor's chosen charity. This time it was for an animal shelter in a neighbouring town. Taking part in the fundraiser would be another opportunity to make sure they became part of the community, and Ellie was certain that people would pay to let their children pet Gerald and some of the other animals, like Dolly the goat.

'That's wonderful news. But more importantly, how was Ben?' Karen gave her a knowing look; it was her turn to tease.

'Fine.' Ellie hesitated. She might as well tell her mother the truth; she had a feeling that Kelsea Bay was the sort of place where news travelled fast. 'Actually, he asked me if I'd like to go to the barn dance with him on Saturday. Apparently there's an amazing hog roast. I wondered if you fancied it too.'

'Absolutely not!' Karen was smiling again. 'Not only have I got two left feet and been known to bring down a whole anniversary reel, but there's absolutely no way I'm going to cramp your style.

Not now you're seeing such a nice chap.'

'I'm not *seeing* him, Mum.' Ellie pulled a face, but Karen just shrugged; she was fighting a losing battle, trying to convince her mother otherwise. 'Can I ask you something, though? You haven't been able to hide your enthusiasm about Ben, but why didn't you ever tell me how you felt about Rupert when we were together?'

'You had to realise for yourself what was the right thing to do. If I'd told you to steer clear of him, you wouldn't have understood why.' Karen squeezed her hand. 'But remember, your old mum knows best, and I think Ben could make you really happy.'

'Mum, I keep telling you I don't want to rush into anything. It's one date, to a barn dance in the village — we're hardly announcing our engagement in *The Times*.'

'Maybe not yet, but Hilary knew what she was doing when she left us this place.' She squeezed Ellie's hand again. 'Just you wait and see.'

5

By the time Saturday rolled around, Ellie had arranged an interview with an employment agency in Elverham, the nearest big town to Kelsea Bay, for the following week. Some temporary office work would tide her over until she found the thing she really wanted to do, whatever that was. The agency had been impressed with her CV and tried to persuade her to go for an interview for a role as events co-ordinator with a large firm of lawyers. The money was good, and it was only half an hour's commute from the farm, but the thought of plunging straight back into the corporate world made her go cold. Despite her growing panic about money, she'd stood her ground and told them that she was definitely only looking for something temporary. She just had to hope they could come up with something before she was forced in a direction she really didn't want.

Karen looked up from the book she was reading and gave Ellie a thumbs-up sign. 'You look amazing. A proper country girl.'

'I don't think the average Kentish farmhand really wears cowboy boots and a pink Stetson, but I'll be able to hoedown with the best of them.' Leaning forward, she kissed her mother on the cheek, breathing in the familiar scent of English fern. 'I won't be late.'

'Be as late as you like, darling, but know that I'll be waiting up anyway.' Karen gave her a little wave. 'I'll want to hear *all* the gossip!'

★   ★   ★

The lights of the church hall were blazing, visible from a good distance away. It wasn't until Ellie got closer that she could make out the unmistakable sound of a barn-dance band. It was a relief to discover that she wasn't the only one to go all out and don country-and-western gear. Ben was outside the double doors waiting for her, wearing a checked shirt and Levi's that were tucked into some very authentic-looking cowboy boots, with silver spurs to finish off the look.

'Howdy there, pretty lady. Y'all here for the dance?' He grinned, immediately dropping his attempt at a southern American twang. 'Sorry, I can't keep that up. The only accent I've ever been able to do is the one I've got.' He took her hand as he spoke and she tried not to think how nice it felt, still determined to keep things casual.

'I'll let you off. I like your normal voice anyway.' She didn't catch his response, as half the town seemed to be in the church hall waiting just to greet Ben. He was the perfect gentleman, and introduced Ellie to everyone who came up to say hello. She was usually good with names — a legacy from her job in events management — but even she was struggling to recall more than three or four; there were just too many new faces to lock them all into her memory bank.

'That's my sister, Daisy.' Ben pointed towards a pretty girl wearing dungarees and a straw hat with two thick blonde plaits poking out from underneath it. She had painted-on freckles and an air of irrepressible enthusiasm as she bounded over to greet them.

'Hi, Daisy. This is my friend, Ellie.' Ben moved aside to let them shake hands, but Daisy immediately enveloped Ellie in a hug.

'Ellie! It's so fabulous to meet you at last. I've heard so much about you.' She stepped back and looked her up and down. 'And for once, Benji boy didn't exaggerate.' Ellie guessed that Daisy must be in her late twenties, but it was hard to tell between the braids and painted-on freckles.

'Daisy, I warned you not to be a blabbermouth! You're not too old for hair-pulling, you know, and those plaits would be perfect — just like the old days!' Ben teased his sister in the way that only a brother could.

'Sorry, sorry, my lips are sealed.' Daisy giggled loudly. 'I'll do things the proper way and not let on how much you keep talking about her.' She turned towards Ellie, giving a little bob of her head. 'Welcome to Kelsea Bay. How are you liking it so far?'

'It's great. We haven't got to know the town as much as we'd like, as we've been so busy sorting things out at the farm.' Ellie paused. She was going to say that everyone had been really friendly so far, but then she remembered Alan Crabtree. 'We love living so near the sea, and I'm sure it's only a matter of time before we feel like part of the community. Ben inviting me here has certainly helped.'

'Ah yes, he can be very helpful when the mood takes him.' Daisy winked, earning herself another nudge in the ribs from her brother. 'Come on then, you two, let's see what you're made of. You've got to work up an appetite for the buffet and the hog roast. There's enough food to last until Christmas by the look of it.'

★   ★   ★

Karen was just settling down to watch *Casualty* when she heard knocking. Someone was at the front door. By now it was dark, and Gerald obviously hadn't spotted the visitor; there'd been no braying to herald the arrival of a stranger in the yard. She suddenly felt nervous; she was home alone, and the farm was a lot more isolated than their old house at The Copse, where the neighbours had only ever been a knock on the wall away. Perhaps they should get a dog when everything was settled and all the fencing had been repaired. The last thing she needed was to have a dog escape into Alan's farm next door and cause havoc. They seemed to have established the beginning of what might be termed a neighbourly relationship, with the exchange of cakes and flowers, but she had no doubt it was just as fragile as the delicate foxgloves he'd left on their doorstep. A marauding hound would soon put paid to any hope she had of building a proper friendship with their new neighbour.

Peering through the peephole in the front door, Karen was more than a little surprised to see the person she'd just been thinking about standing there. And if she was honest, she was relieved too. Alan Crabtree might not be the friendliest person in the world, but at least it wasn't a complete stranger waiting outside her door in the dark.

'Mr Crabtree, come in.' She held open the door and he moved past her, a large parcel in his arms.

'Alan, please.' He smiled, and for the first time she noticed how green his eyes were and how different he looked when his mouth was turned upwards. He should smile more often. 'Shall I put this on the table?'

'Yes, yes of course.'

She pushed the recipe books she'd

left spread out on the kitchen table to one side. She'd meant to put them away before she'd settled down to watch television, but these days it was rare to have complete control of the remote and watch the programmes she wanted to watch on a Saturday night. Ellie liked those dating shows full of canned laughter and over-the-top banter between the contestants, but Karen couldn't stand them. Romance should be old-fashioned, like delivering flowers to the doorstep. Even as the notion entered her head, she felt embarrassed at having thought it.

'Well, if you're to be Alan, then I insist you call me Karen. Mrs Chapman makes me sound like my former mother-in-law, and let's just say that she wasn't the most likeable of people.'

'Karen it is, then.' Alan smiled again, and the transformation on his face was undeniable. Perhaps she was imagining it, but he looked different altogether — close-shaven, and even his nails were spotlessly clean; a rarity for a potato farmer like him, she'd bet.

'Neighbours should be on first-name terms.' She returned his smile, almost reluctant to ask him the reason for his visit in case it broke the spell and he turned back into Mr Grumpy. Still, it was a bit awkward just standing there, so in the end she had to ask. 'It's lovely to see you, but I was just wondering what brought you here at this time on a Saturday evening.'

'Sadly, it's a long time since Saturday evenings had any significance for me.' He laughed and she knew the surprise at his candour must have shown on her face. 'Don't look so worried. I came because of the parcel.' He gestured towards the package that he'd just placed on her table, and it was her turn to laugh. She'd forgotten about him struggling in with that, in all the shock of it being him at the door.

'Oh gosh, I hadn't realised that was for us.' Karen leant forward to look at the label, racking her brain as to what it might be.

'Bill, the postie, asked if I'd take it in for you. Apparently you weren't in the house when he knocked and he thought it might be something you needed urgently.' Alan gave a casual shrug. 'It was no bother for me to bring it over, and it's a heck of a drive to the sorting office in Elverham just to pick it up.'

'That's so kind of you.' Karen pulled a chair out from the kitchen table and indicated that Alan should sit down. 'Can I persuade you to stay for a cup of tea? I was just about to make one.' It wasn't strictly true but as far as Karen was concerned, there was always time for a cuppa.

'Well, I . . . ' He looked as though he was desperately trying to think up a plausible excuse, and she hated seeing him so uncomfortable.

'Of course, if you've got somewhere else to be, I completely understand. But if it does anything to persuade you, I've got some freshly baked Eccles cakes on the cooling rack.'

'Like I said, my Saturday nights have

been free for a long time, and I never could say no to an Eccles cake.' He took the seat that Karen had offered. 'They were always your aunt's speciality, you know.'

'She taught me to make them when I couldn't even reach the kitchen counter. They were her fiancé's favourite, so she told me, and she made them every weekend without fail, as if she still expected him to pop round and ask for one. She wanted a batch ready, just in case.'

Karen busied herself filling the kettle, but when she looked across at Alan she could see he was watching her intently.

'She was a fine woman, your Aunt Hilary. I can see a lot of her in you.' It was meant as a compliment and she dropped her gaze, not sure how to respond at first.

'It's funny that we never met,' she said, 'since I spent so much time here over the years and you were just next door.'

'I wasn't good with strangers.' Alan sighed. 'My mum was a bit too trusting, and then something happened that made me all the more wary.' He paused for a moment as though he was about to say something else, but seemed to think better of it.

'I'm sure you had your reasons.' Karen filled the teapot. She didn't want to push him. The progress they'd made over the last couple of days at becoming good neighbours — if not good friends — was frankly incredible. 'How do you take your tea?'

'With milk, no sugar, and two Eccles cakes.' He smiled, which lit up his face again.

'Coming right up.' She glanced at the clock; it was nine fifteen. By the time she looked at it again it was ten thirty. If someone had told her the day before that she'd pass over an hour in easy conversation with Alan Crabtree, she'd have called them crazy. As it was, it had turned out to be one of the most enjoyable evenings she'd spent in a long time. She only hoped that Ellie was having as much fun.

*   *   *

Ellie half-collapsed onto one of the hay bales that were set in a rectangle around the inside of the church hall, her face flushed from twirling around the floor with so many partners during the mixer. Her head was still spinning when she sat down.

'Having a good time?' Ben handed her a cool glass of cloudy lemonade that he'd got from the makeshift bar at one end of the hall.

'I really am.' She took a sip of her drink, which tingled on her tongue. 'This is delicious, and just what I needed.'

'We aim to please, madam.' He gave her a mock bow. 'It's the least I can do, considering how many times I've stepped on your feet this evening.'

'You're in luck.' She laughed at the genuine look of concern on his face. 'I think these cowboy boots were designed with buffalo ranching in mind, and I don't think even a charging herd of cattle trampling over my feet would register in these things!'

'Just as well, because I was hoping it wouldn't put you off coming out with me again.'

She was about to answer when Daisy bounded over. Ellie had no idea where Ben's sister got her energy from, but despite leading every dance it didn't show any sign of waning.

'Grub's up, Benji.' She yanked her brother's arm. 'We've got to show Ellie how we do hospitality in Kelsea Bay, and Nathan is in charge of the hog roast, so he's promised to save us the best bits of crackling.'

'We've had the royal command.' Ben gave Ellie an apologetic shrug. 'And if you think Daisy is full-on, just wait until you meet Nathan. You'll do well to get a word in edgeways between the two of them.'

The hog roast and buffet had been set up in an open-sided marquee just outside the church hall. If the smell wafting in through the open skylights whilst they'd been dancing was any-thing to go by, they were in for a treat. The buffet table was heaving with food;

Daisy hadn't been exaggerating. There were at least six different types of salad for a start, and potatoes cooked four different ways. Loaves of French bread were stacked on top of one another, a crusty avalanche just waiting to happen. There was a separate table laden with desserts too — cheesecakes, chocolate brownies and cupcakes thick with icing, which looked capable of rivalling something Karen would produce.

'Ah, Benji boy, there you are!' A tall sandy-haired man waved a large pair of serving tongs in their faces as they finally made it to the front of the queue. 'No wonder you've been keeping this lovely lady all to yourself. If I wasn't an engaged man, you'd have to watch out. I'm Nathan, by the way.' He wiped his hand on his apron and held it out to Ellie.

'It's lovely to meet you. I'm Ellie Chapman. My mother and I recently moved into Channel View Farm.'

'We all know who *you* are.' Nathan gave her a leisurely smile, immediately putting her at her ease. The flirting was clearly just part of his charm, and Daisy certainly didn't seem to mind. 'You're all Benji can talk about these days.'

'Really?' It was the second time she'd been told that in one evening, and she turned to Ben, who attempted a casual shrug. He'd already said he wanted to see her again, so perhaps there was some truth in what Nathan and Daisy had been saying — though she was pretty certain they were laying it on thick, just to embarrass him.

'That's not strictly true.' Ben picked up two plates and passed one to her. 'I've also been talking about this highly anticipated hog roast. Nathan's an architect by trade, but it's his first year in charge of the roast, and he fancies himself as a bit of a Michelin-starred chef when it comes to barbecuing.'

'You're such a philistine, Ben.' Nathan used his tongs to pull some pork from the spit and loaded up their plates. 'Hog roasts and barbecues are, at best, distantly related cousins. Luckily for you, I'm a master at both.'

* ★ ★

As it turned out, Nathan was as good as his word. The pork was delicious, and the rest of the buffet didn't disappoint. At least not until Ellie sampled two of the desserts; neither of them tasted as good as they looked, and the cupcakes felt like sawdust in her mouth, they were so dry. Perhaps it was just because she'd been spoilt by her mum's brilliant baking; but looking round, there were plates of abandoned desserts everywhere — half-eaten cupcakes and chocolate brownies with only a forkful taken out of them.

'Not quite up to your mum's standard are they?' Ben set down his barely touched cheesecake on the table closest to their hay bale.

'I didn't like to say anything in case they'd been made by one of your friends.' Ellie breathed a sigh of relief that Ben had mentioned it first and put down her plate next to his.

'Not a friend, no, but they all come

from Daisy's deli; everything in the buffet does.'

Even though he laughed, she wanted the ground to open up and swallow her, hay bale and all. 'Mum and Daisy run it together, but since the lady who used to supply all their homemade desserts moved to Devon last month, they just haven't been able to find a reliable supplier. Don't tell anyone, but most of this stuff comes from a frozen-food firm. The cupcakes were from a new supplier they were hoping would work out, but I think we can safely say that isn't the case.'

'I'm sorry. I wouldn't have said anything, and I'm sure it's not really that bad.' Ellie looked at her abandoned dessert again, wondering if she could force down a mouthful.

'You only said what everyone else is thinking, Mum and Daisy included. They're both great at cooking the savoury stuff, but desserts just don't seem to be their forte, and so they've always bought those in.' He gave her a rueful smile. 'If only we knew someone who was a dab hand at knocking up a sponge cake.'

'Do you think they'd give Mum a trial — if she was prepared to give it a go, I mean?' Ellie felt a frisson of excitement. Being a regular supplier to a well-established deli like Daisy's could be just the way to expand Karen's business.

'I think they'd jump at the chance. I could bring Daisy up to try out some of your mum's cakes next week, if you think she'll be interested.' He slid an arm around her shoulders. 'And maybe afterwards I could take you out for that second date.'

'That would be lovely.' Ellie leant against Ben's shoulder as couples promenaded past them, following the band leader's commands. Dodgy desserts aside, life in Kelsea Bay was shaping up to be everything that Ellie had hoped for; and, try as she might to tell herself she wasn't interested in a relationship, it seemed as though fate had other ideas.

6

It was so hot in the kitchen that Karen had opened all the windows; her cheeks were flushed as red as the strawberry jam in the tray of tarts she'd just removed from the oven. Every spare surface was covered in trays of cooling cakes and pastries.

'Tea?' Ellie wanted to do something to help, but Karen was rushing around like a whirling dervish and she shook her head at the offer of a drink. Her mum saying no to a cuppa meant things were really serious, and she wondered if she'd been wrong to put her under so much pressure. 'It'll be okay, Mum. Even if they don't want your cakes for the deli, I'm sure you'll soon have some new clients lined up. Wedding season is about to get underway, after all.'

'The bills keep coming in, though, Ellie.' Karen took another tray of golden fairy cakes out of the oven as she spoke. The delicious smell of vanilla filled the air.

'The employment agency seems certain it'll find me some work next week,' Ellie said. 'And if I have to, I'll get something permanent. I don't want you worrying about money, Mum. You've sacrificed enough, putting all the cash you got for the old house into this place. I'll worry about the rest.' She crossed her fingers behind her back, hoping that it would be as simple as that. They were okay for now, but maintaining things on the farm would continue to cost a lot of money, and they'd need to find a long-term solution eventually. Still, that was a worry for another day. Today their job was to impress Daisy. Ben's mum had stayed behind to manage the deli, so the entire decision rested with his sister. Ellie had met their mum, Joy, at the barn dance; she was quiet and soft-spoken, and it was clear that Daisy was the driving force in the business, the one who made all the decisions.

It was almost a relief when the distinctive crunch of tyres on gravel heralded Ben and Daisy's arrival. They'd done all they could do to prepare for the grand tasting session, and perhaps Karen would be able to relax once she'd met Daisy and realised how friendly she was.

Ben's sister breezed into the room and made herself at home immediately, sitting down at the kitchen table before she was even invited to do so. 'It's a lovely place you've got here. And the smell of all this baking is just divine — we were getting it from halfway down the drive.'

'I'll put the kettle on, and you can decide what you want to try first.' Karen moved towards the other end of the kitchen and Ellie could see that her hands were shaking. It was odd to think of her mum feeling nervous. She'd held their little family together for so long that she'd always seemed invincible to Ellie.

Ben took a seat opposite Daisy and next to Ellie. 'I can recommend the gypsy tart,' he said.

'Help yourself then, Ben. Someone needs to dig in.' Karen didn't join them at the table, clearly too anxious to sit down herself. She'd never had a contract as big as the one that Daisy's deli could potentially offer, and Ellie knew as well as she did that there was a lot riding on Daisy's verdict.

Ellie took one of the cakes, peeling back the paper and revealing an inch and a half of perfect golden sponge with another inch of expertly swirled icing resting on top. 'Mum's cupcakes are the best I've ever tasted, and that's not bias talking.'

'They do look incredible.' Daisy helped herself to a cake from the same plate as Ellie. 'What flavours do you make?'

'I've made almost everything over the years,' Karen told her, 'from banana to lemon, carrot to chocolate, coffee to strawberry, and everything in between.

I even made walnut and lime once — not a combination I'd ever thought of, but it was the bride's favourite. And what a bride says goes on her big day.'

'Oh wow!' Daisy spoke with her mouth full. 'This sponge is so light. But please tell me I didn't mishear you . . . do you really make wedding cakes too?'

Karen nodded and Daisy had crossed the room in a flash, flinging her arms around the older woman.

'I take it you like the cakes as much as I said you would,' Ben laughed. Karen looked a bit dazed from being on the receiving end of one of Daisy's enthusiastic reactions.

'You didn't tell me she made wedding cakes, Ben! You know how stressed I've been about the plans for the wedding. Nothing seems to be going right; all I've got so far is a theme and the dress. Being able to tick the cake off my list would be at least one step in the right direction.' Daisy finally let go of Karen. 'And now it looks very much like I've found my wedding cake designer, as well as a new supplier for the deli.'

Ellie, who couldn't imagine Daisy ever truly getting stressed, was glad of the opportunity to make herself useful at last. Disappearing into the lounge as the others tucked into more of her mum's samples, she quickly returned with a small photo album, which she set down in front of Ben's sister.

'There are pictures in there of some of Mum's celebration cakes. They're mostly weddings, but there are some birthday and anniversary cakes too. It'll give you an idea of what she can do.'

For once, Daisy was silent as she flicked through the album. Ellie felt prouder of her mum than ever, watching Daisy's face as she took in each new photograph.

'These are amazing. Are the flowers real?' Daisy pointed to a three-tier cake that had a waterfall of daisies cascading all down one side.

'No, I made them from icing sugar.'

Karen smiled. 'The groom proposed on a picnic by threading the engagement ring onto a daisy chain and presenting it to his bride-to-be. They wanted it to be captured in the wedding cake somehow, so I came up with this design.'

'Could you do something like this for me? Maybe with a little cottage on top to represent the design Nathan has done for our first home, with a garden full of wild daisies?' Daisy clapped her hands together in delight as Karen nodded.

'I think,' said Ben, taking another slice of gypsy tart, 'that this is cause for celebration, and the only way to mark it appropriately is to have another piece of cake.'

* * *

Within an hour, they'd made pretty impressive inroads into Karen's samples, and Daisy had settled on a final design for the wedding cake.

Ben sat back in his chair and massaged his stomach. 'I don't know about you, but I could do with walking some of these calories off. A brisk walk to John O'Groats and back again should just about do it.'

'I'm not sure if I can commit to that.' Ellie laughed. 'But I need to go down to the starvation paddock and check on Gerald.' They'd moved him down to the far end of the farm. Alan had come over with one of his tractors and cut the grass as short as an army crew cut to ensure that the old donkey couldn't overeat and risk getting laminitis again. His willingness to help had shocked Ellie, but Karen hadn't seemed nearly as surprised. Ellie was sure something else had happened after the mysterious appearance of the foxgloves on the doorstep, but they'd both been too busy to talk about it properly. The decision to move Gerald further away from the house had been taken, at least in part, to help Karen avoid the temptation of feeding him titbits. His mournful braying wasn't easy to resist, and since her mother had always equated feeding people with love, Ellie had decided it was best for them both to move Gerald out of earshot.

'Would you mind if I tagged along too?' Daisy grinned, obviously deciding to ignore the warning look her brother had shot her. 'I haven't seen any of the donkeys since Hilary shut the sanctuary down, and I used to love coming here.'

'Of course not.' Ellie got to her feet and pulled on the light summer jacket she'd draped over the back of her chair. 'We've started to replace the fencing and we've done a lot of tidying up on the farm, but we've still got a way to go. Our neighbour, Alan, has been really helpful lately, though. Hasn't he, Mum?' As Ellie spoke Karen nodded, but she didn't seem keen to elaborate and was saved from having to do so by an interjection from Ben's sister.

'Alan Crabtree has been *helpful*? Without a gun to his head?' Daisy looked incredulous. 'Mind you, having tasted your cakes, I think you might just have the sort of magical powers it would take to bring about a miracle like that.'

* * *

The trees that marked the end of the farm, and which were just out of reach of Gerald's starvation paddock, were heavy with blossom. It was a beautiful afternoon in mid-May, and the sea was as calm as a millpond at the base of the cliffs. The view was so clear that it looked as if France was close enough to swim to, although the reality was very different of course.

'He looks well.' Ben held out a hand to stroke the donkey's ear. Gerald regarded him with a knowing look, as if he realised it was Ben who was responsible for his spartan diet. 'Are you still restricting him to a pad of hay a day?'

'Yes, exactly as the doctor ordered.' Ellie glanced at Ben and they exchanged a smile.

'It's beautiful here,' Daisy said. 'It never really struck me before. I suppose you don't notice those things as much when you're a child.' She stood on the other side of her brother, leaning against the top rail of Gerald's paddock and looking out towards the sea. 'If you had a gazebo over there at the end of the woodland, with the view of the sea and France beyond it as a backdrop, it would make a stunning venue for a wedding. You could use the hay barn for indoor ceremonies — that sort of thing is really popular now. I've looked at loads, but nothing as nice as this. The barn would work for receptions too, or you could pitch a huge marquee close to the cliff top.' She had that dreamy look that lots of brides seemed to get, as if she really could visualise it all.

'Do you really think people would want to get married here?' Ellie was suddenly seeing the farm through fresh eyes. It was a real possibility, and she couldn't believe she'd never thought of it before. The barn was probably in better condition than the farmhouse, and it had beautiful oak beams that would look stunning hung with floral displays. It wouldn't take that much to bring it up to scratch, not in the grand scheme of things, compared with the money they'd already spent on the farm.

'You'd be run off your feet with bookings,' Daisy went on. 'Your mum could do the wedding cakes and desserts, and the deli could supply the rest of the catering.' Her enthusiasm was infectious. She spoke as though it was already a reality — just as simple as saying so.

'That's always been my dream job, being a wedding planner,' Ellie said. 'I love the idea of being part of the most important day of someone's life.' She was starting to visualise it too. Just maybe it was doable, even if she had no idea of the practicalities it would involve.

'Leave you two alone together and you'd be ruling the world within half a day.' If Ben was trying to sound a gentle warning note, it had fallen on deaf ears.

'Come on, let's see what you need to do to register it as a venue,' Daisy said.

'I take it you've got Wi-Fi?' She had already linked her arm through Ellie's and was heading back toward the house. 'I'll tell you something — if you can get the approval in time for my wedding at the beginning of September, I'll be first in the queue. We might even get our pictures in *Kent Life*.' She picked up the pace, leaving Ben trailing in their wake. 'Keep up, we've got loads to organise!'

*　*　*

It had been the sort of day that changed everything. Not since discovering they'd inherited the farm from Aunt Hilary had so much happened at once. First there was the offer of a contract at the deli and the commissioning of Daisy's wedding cake. Now Ellie and Daisy were back at the house, looking into how to register the farm as a wedding venue. It was exciting, but exhausting. Just listening to the pace of the conversation had Karen feeling worn out. Ben had disappeared to take evening surgery at his veterinary practice, and she'd taken the opportunity to escape too. It was staying light until almost nine p.m., but by the time she set off towards the cliffs for five minutes of quiet contemplation, the pink sky was fading slowly to a deep mauve.

It was easy to see why Hilary had loved the farm so much. Where the land ended, a vast sea stretched out, and it almost felt as though you owned it all. Daisy was right, it would make a stunning venue for a wedding, and Karen could just imagine what Ellie would achieve with it. It could be her dream come true.

There was a large, flat rock next to the gatepost in Gerald's bald little paddock. The old donkey was scuffing his mouth against the ground, getting what little grass he could between his teeth. Karen knew they had to be cruel to be kind, and as hard as that sometimes was, she could admit he was looking much healthier. She'd even seen him kick up his back legs in response to a horse fly landing on his rump — something he would never have been able to do a month before.

The rock was the perfect place to sit and just think, the sky gradually darkening from mauve to plum. Her mind drifted, imagining how pleased her aunt would have been to see the farm used for weddings. Hilary was a person who believed in one true love for each person — soulmates; so much so that she'd never even considered finding someone else after she'd lost her fiancé.

A lump formed in Karen's throat as she thought about her own wedding. She'd truly believed it was love, back then at least. But she knew for certain now that it wasn't. She was fifty-five years old and she'd never really been cherished by someone the way that Hilary and Gerald had loved one another. It was stupid to cry over things like that at her age, she chided herself. But rational as she tried to be, it still hurt. Thank heavens Ellie had seen the light and finished with Rupert — he'd never have cherished her either. The only person Rupert loved was himself. Karen wanted the best for her daughter — a partner whose eyes lit up every time she entered the room; and she could see that when Ben looked at Ellie, in a way Rupert never had.

'Did you know that when you left us the farm? That somehow you'd break the hold Rupert had over her?' Karen whispered the words into the still night air; and in the quickly descending darkness, she could just make out Gerald's ear twitching in response.

Suddenly his head shot upwards as a loud cracking sound came from the woods at the other side of his paddock, as if someone had snapped a branch in two. She stood up from the rock and took her torch out of her pocket, shining it towards the woods, suddenly aware of her heart hammering in her chest. The beam from the torch was weak and it was getting really dark, but for a moment she thought she saw two figures standing on the edge of the woodland, one of whom looked familiar. She rubbed her eyes, wondering if she was seeing things, and when she opened them again there was no one there. Maybe it was the dark playing tricks on her — trees looking a bit like people — but she could have sworn she'd caught a glimpse of Rupert. It must have been her imagination, though, because he'd been on her mind. Why on earth would anyone be lurking in the woods, let alone Rupert of all people? Adrenaline was rushing through her veins all the same, and it no longer seemed such a good idea to be sitting alone on the edge of a cliff as the sky turned darker still.

Turning, she pointed her torch towards the path. It flickered for a second or two and then went out, the batteries dying to nothing. By now it was hard to see where she was stepping, and in her haste to get back to the welcoming lights of the farmhouse she caught her ankle on a tree root, hurtling forwards in the dark. She was going to hit the ground any second and it was going to hurt. Except she didn't. Something, or someone, had caught hold of her, steadying her for a moment and then letting her go.

'Are you okay?' The deep voice was familiar, and she let out the breath she hadn't realised she'd been holding.

'Alan! I was scared half to death for a moment there.'

'I was going to call out when I saw you, but then you tripped and there wasn't time. Sorry.' He sounded out of breath himself; he must have shot towards her with lightning speed when he'd seen her about to fall.

'Don't be sorry. I'm just so relieved it was you.' She took his arm to steady herself again, still shaken by tripping and the fright of what she thought she'd seen back at the woods. 'It seems like you're destined to be my hero, always turning up when I'm in danger. You must have some kind of sixth sense.'

'Not really.' He gave a low laugh and

she thought briefly how much she enjoyed hearing the sound. 'Last time I was the one presenting the danger by knocking on your door so late at night. And this time I'm here because I phoned and spoke to Ellie, who told me you'd gone for a walk. I wanted to know how it had gone with Daisy this afternoon. When I rang back twenty minutes later and Ellie said you were still out, I got a bit worried, so I thought I'd head over and see if you were okay.'

'You might pretend to be all bluster and disinterest, Alan Crabtree, but I know your secret now.' She squeezed his arm as she spoke. It was nice to have someone to lean on for a change.

'Not many people do, so I'd rather you kept that to yourself.' There was a teasing tone to his voice. 'You should be a bit more careful, though. If you'd fallen out here in the dark and hit your head, it doesn't bear thinking about. You were hurtling back towards the house like a sprinter, and running in the pitch black is never a good idea.'

'I thought I saw someone . . . something down on the edge of the woods.' She shivered at the memory. 'But it must have just been a trick of the fading light or the shadows of the trees.'

'Are you sure? I can check it out if you like.' He swung round in the direction of the woods, but it was now too dark for Karen to even make out his features clearly, and he was standing right next to her.

'Maybe tomorrow? You could come over and I'll do you a bit of lunch.' She already felt better at the prospect of putting her mind at rest, with Alan there to talk her out of all this nonsense she'd been imagining. One thing you could rely on him to do was to tell things straight. 'But for now, let's head to the house and see if those girls have left us anything to eat. I'm sure you could use a cuppa as much as I can.'

'It sounds like a pretty good plan to me.' Linking his arm back through hers, they made their way towards the farmhouse, thoughts of Rupert and his possible appearance at the edge of the woodland temporarily forgotten.

7

Being back in an office environment felt like torture to Ellie after the freedom of the farm. The warm weather had continued into late June, and she wished for the first time in her life that she had a desk facing a wall rather than looking out onto everything she was missing.

Cooper and Co. was a large firm of accountants situated right next to a public park in Elverham. The employment agency had got Ellie a month's contract helping one of the partners out with a new marketing campaign, but trying to make taxation services sound exciting was almost a challenge too far. When her mind wandered from the advertising campaign, which it frequently did, she found herself watching mums with their little ones playing in the park. They wheeled their pushchairs in the sunshine and fed the ducks in the large pond that dominated the centre of the park, making Ellie wish she could be back at the farm with her own little family.

Family . . . For so long it had just been Ellie and her mum — along with Aunt Hilary and her grandparents, of course — but it felt like that little unit was starting to extend. Gerald the ancient donkey, Dolly the goat, and the other animals in the menagerie were like part of the family too, almost as if Aunt Hilary was still with them. Then there was Alan Crabtree, who Ellie had genuinely grown fond of over the few months since their first meeting back in March. He'd helped them so much with getting the farm straight, and Ellie had never seen her mum laugh as often as when Alan was around. Then there was Ben and his family. Her relationship with Ben was still in its early days, but if she couldn't yet admit to loving him, she certainly loved being around him and his family. Daisy and Nathan were both full of energy; and while his parents were quieter, they were just as welcoming of Ellie into their lives.

Karen's baking for the deli was selling, somewhat ironically, like hotcakes, and that had really helped establish them in Kelsea Bay too. Ellie had also applied for a grant of approval from the council to establish Channel View Farm as a licenced venue for civil weddings. Since then, they'd been working really hard to make sure it was ready for inspection and met health and safety regulations. Alan had started on the construction of a gazebo, too, for outside ceremonies. Ellie was keeping her fingers crossed that it would all be approved in time for Daisy's wedding, especially as she was doing absolutely nothing else to secure a different venue as a backup plan. Ben's sister was one of those upbeat people who just put their faith in everything turning out okay, and she had assured everyone that it almost always did. But that didn't stop Ellie waking up in the night sometimes, wondering what on earth they would do if the council turned down their application. In the meantime, they'd provisionally booked a registrar, and Daisy was poised to send out invitations as soon as they got the official go-ahead.

It couldn't come a moment too soon for Ellie. For her, running a wedding venue at the farm was equivalent to winning the lottery. She knew they'd need a healthy slush fund in the early days to keep the farm afloat. The money from the old house and her redundancy had dwindled fast, especially with the work they'd had to do to make the barn a stand-out wedding venue, and even with Alan putting in all the hours that God sent and refusing to take anything for it. In the meantime, Ellie had no choice but to take the temporary contracts the employment agency offered her. She was about to finish her month-long stint with Cooper and Co., hoping against hope the agency would come up with something a little less dull this time.

When her mobile rang on her last afternoon at the accountant's, she would have bet her last pound on it being the agency with details of her latest assignment. But it was Ben.

'Have you accepted a job for next week yet?' He didn't start with his normal *hello* or *how are you*, and he sounded uncharacteristically stressed.

'No, I'm just waiting for the agency to ring. In fact, I thought your call was going to be them.'

'Thank God.' He let out a long breath. 'My receptionist has put her back out, and I know it's a bit more basic than the sort of work you normally do, but I wondered if you'd step in. I need someone reliable first thing on Monday morning. I'd pay you the going rate for a temp, of course. And I'm desperate.'

'Saying that you're desperate is not the way to convince a woman she's the one for you.' Ellie laughed, but if he'd been there she'd have hugged him. The pay might not be as good as the work the agency could get her in events or marketing, but working in Kelsea Bay with Ben was well worth the pay cut. 'Still, seeing as you asked so nicely, how can I say no?'

'Really?' He sounded as though he

couldn't quite believe his luck. 'I could kiss you!'

'Maybe later, Mr Hastings. Although now that you're my boss, I'm not sure that's appropriate anymore.'

'I'll add to the job description in that case. You're one in a million, Ellie — you know that, don't you?' His voice was warm and she could picture his dark brown eyes twinkling as he spoke, half of her wishing it was already Monday morning.

'So I've been told. I'll see you later, boss.' She put down the phone, stood up and did a little dance around the office. Goodbye, Cooper and Co. Things were looking up.

* * *

The stile that crossed into Crabtree Farm came into view and Karen smiled to herself, thinking about the first time she'd climbed over it, carrying a huge cake box whilst Alan did his best to ignore her. Now he was already waiting to help her over it, and not just because he didn't want his beloved Eccles cakes to get squashed. He'd been more helpful than she could ever have imagined since that night he'd brought over the package he'd taken off the postman for her. The day after she thought she'd seen Rupert down at the woods, hed gone to check it out, and then reassured her that there was no sign anyone had been down there; it was still as overgrown with brambles and trees as it had always been. The only trace of anyone ever having been there was a patch of green material caught on one of the spikier branches. They both said it could have been there for years, and it was ridiculous to think that Rupert might have been lurking about anyway. He'd never exactly been shy when it came to getting what he wanted. If he'd wanted to see Ellie, he'd have just turned up at their door.

The gazebo Alan was building was taking shape nicely too. It was hexagonal with ornately carved struts, a low fence with vertical posts, and a red tiled roof. He'd made some rails inside, where swathes of organza could be hung, and Ellie was planning to start painting the woodwork in antique cream on her next weekend off. Karen had wanted to find a way to thank him after he'd refused to accept any money, so in her usual manner she'd shown her appreciation through food. Making sure the farm ticked over while Ellie was at work and keeping up with the demands from the deli kept her busy enough, but she could always find time to make Alan his favourite things. She'd taken to cooking for him every lunchtime, whether he was working on something at Channel View Farm or on his own land, and sharing a meal with him every day meant that they'd grown much closer over the weeks. Yet she still didn't know the whole story; still didn't know why he put up the façade he presented to almost everyone. Especially when, at heart, he was one of the kindest men Karen had ever known.

'I've got your favourites today.' She accepted his hand as he helped her over the stile and didn't object when he kept hold of it. 'Thick-cut ham on fresh brown bread and a nice Eccles cake for afterwards.'

'And a flask of tea if I know you, Karen Chapman.' He grinned and she nodded. He'd joked more than once that they should change the words of the nursery rhyme so it said 'Karen put the kettle on' instead of Polly.

Alan had set up a little makeshift picnic area using some bales of straw, from which he'd fashioned two seats and a table of sorts. The weather had been so good of late that they'd both agreed it was too nice to waste by having lunch indoors.

'So what have you been up to today?' Karen asked as Alan eagerly tucked into his sandwich, waiting while he finished his mouthful.

'I've been planting trees down at the far end of the farm, where it borders the caravan park.' He said the words 'caravan park' much like someone might say 'sewer works', as if the two things were on a par as far as he was concerned. 'A few of the trees that screen it from the farm came down last winter. I like to be able to see as little of that place as possible, so I've replaced the missing trees with some mature fir trees I had delivered that are already eight feet tall. They cost me a fortune, but they were worth every penny.'

'Is that why you aren't keen on strangers, having a holiday park so close by?' It had never looked like a rowdy sort of place when Karen had driven past it, but maybe it was different when you lived right next door.

'It's not so much the people who are there now. But the memories of how the place got set up mean I can't bear to look at it.' He put his sandwich down as he spoke, as if talking about the caravan park had robbed him of his appetite. 'I suppose you want to know the whole story.'

'Only if you want to tell me.' Karen had never been the sort to push people into confiding in her, but she hoped Alan would. She hoped that their friendship was good enough for that.

'I find myself wanting to tell you everything.' He took her hand across the straw-bale table, his green eyes meeting hers. 'My mother was a wonderful woman — too wonderful for her own good in many ways. She saw the good in everyone, trusted what people said to her as the truth, and in the end she paid the price. When I was growing up, it meant that a few things happened that shouldn't have done. She'd get ripped off when mechanics came to work on the tractors, that sort of thing. Or get a lower price for the potatoes than she could have done. My dad had a weak heart and took a back seat in things. Neither of them had had much schooling either, and they didn't read as well as they might. So it fell to me to look out for their interests.'

'That must have been hard for a young lad.' Karen squeezed his hand, encouraging him to go on.

'It was, and it meant I was distrustful of people, which must have looked to others like I was standoffish. It took me a long time even to trust your Aunt Hilary, though once I got to know her I realised she had a heart of gold — just like her niece.' Their eyes met again, and Karen couldn't deny that what she felt for Alan had shifted beyond friendship a while back.

'I know she was fond of you too, and of your parents,' she said.

'For a long time I managed to keep the people who wanted to take advantage of my parents at bay. Having genuine friends like Hilary helped with that. But of course people have their own lives to live, and when I got to my early twenties I wanted to start living mine.' Alan cast his eyes downward. 'It was selfish of me, knowing how much my parents needed me, and it was something we all suffered for in the end.'

'What happened?' As Karen spoke she felt Alan's grip on her hand tighten.

'I dug irrigation ditches in Africa for a volunteer project organised by a charity that the farmers' union supported. I wanted to see a bit of life; experience the world outside Kelsea Bay.'

'That doesn't sound selfish to me.' Karen kept hold of his hand. The regret in Alan's voice was obvious, though.

'Oh, but it was. I left Mum and Dad to it. While I was away, some chap visited the farm and told them he worked for an organisation that could offer them a way of releasing part of their capital to upgrade the farm equipment. They thought it was some sort of government grant.' Alan gave a deep sigh. 'Of course, it wasn't. Just a shady chancer who'd got them to sell off almost a third of the land in return for a nominal payment — less than you'd get for a barren piece of scrubland, never mind for prime arable land.'

'Wasn't there anything you could do?' Karen could feel her scalp prickling at the thought of someone as vulnerable as Alan's mother being taken advantage of.

'We tried. I came home from Africa straight away and did everything I could think of to try and put it right. We lost a small fortune fighting it through the courts. But because the company had been paid for the land — no matter how small an amount, and because Mum was too proud to admit she could barely read, the court found in his favour.' Alan cleared his throat, emotion almost getting the better of him. 'The thing that galls me most of all was that he didn't even want to farm. The firm he worked for sold off the land to a developer within months of the court case concluding, and eventually planning permission was given for the caravan park. I'm sure everything it put my parents through was what made them ill.'

'Not everyone's like the man who defrauded your parents,' Karen spoke softly. Alan had missed out on so much by closing himself off from the world over the years.

'I know that now. After what happened, I just forgot how to differentiate the good people from the bad — until you came along.' Wrapping his half-eaten sandwich back up, he put it in the picnic basket. 'Do you fancy a walk? We could go somewhere different to finish lunch.'

Nodding as he picked up the basket, Karen took his other hand in hers. They crossed the field to the point where the woodland started. Both farms had a small patch of dense woodland in one corner, which marked the point where the cliff edge fell away most steeply. The patch of woodland was only about two hundred feet deep at Channel View, and Karen assumed the same was true of Crabtree Farm.

They didn't speak as Alan led them down a cleared pathway through the trees. At first the canopy of leaves made it dark, but the dappled sunlight started to get stronger the further down the path they went. Suddenly, with only that subtle warning, they emerged into a large clearing in the woods. The ground was alive with colour: thousands of wildflowers fought for attention, standing tall as if each was trying to outdo the other to get to the sunlight first.

'It's beautiful, Alan.' Karen turned towards him as he set down the basket; their faces were only inches apart. Very slowly, very tenderly, in the middle of the sea of wildflowers, Alan kissed her; and she knew for the first time in her life that someone loved her the way Hilary had loved her fiancé.

'I wanted to show it to you. I've never shown anyone before.' He held her face in his hands as he spoke. 'I cleared the land, knowing it was hidden away from prying eyes and could never be found by accident. I scattered thousands of wildflower seeds so I could have a place to remember Mum and Dad, and they flourished beyond my wildest dreams. It's always been a place of beauty I could escape to when the rest of the world only seemed to offer its ugly side.'

'Thank you for sharing it with me.' It must have taken a lot for him to show her the clearing and tell the story about what had happened to the farm, and to him. But she was glad he had. Now everything made so much more sense.

⋆ ⋆ ⋆

'Do you fancy coming up to Julian London's place with me?' Ben perched on the edge of the reception desk while Ellie filed the last of the case notes away. It was Friday afternoon, and the end of her first week as a temporary veterinary receptionist.

'Is that the sheep farm on the way out to Elverham?' She smiled when he nodded. 'Well, I had thought you might suggest a nice meal or a trip to the cinema, but I suppose this is country life.'

'Julian's invited us to dinner.'

'Us?' If felt as though her eyebrows had shot up into her fringe as she said the word.

'Yes, us. There's no problem with that, is there?' He was teasing her, but she shook her head anyway. 'Well, that's good, because as far as I'm concerned

130

there's very much an 'us', and I thought it would be good for you to meet Julian whilst you're working here. He's one of our most regular clients, and we were best friends at school. I'm often up at the farm; no doubt he'll have me looking at some of the ewes whilst I'm up there tonight.'

'Umm, an evening of sheep husbandry. It's certainly different to how I used to spend my Friday nights when I worked in London.'

'And how was that?' Ben stood up, slipping his arms around her waist as he spoke.

'Oh I don't know . . . in some wine bar, with loads of boring corporate types.' Ellie relaxed into his arms.

'Any regrets?'

'Not one.'

★   ★   ★

Coppergate sheep farm was about five miles outside of Kelsea Bay, and the farmhouse itself was down a long, bumpy track that cut a swath between two small hills. By the time they reached the farm, kangarooing down the track in Ben's four-wheel-drive truck, Ellie felt as though she'd spent ten minutes inside a cocktail shaker.

'Evening, Ben!' A tall, wiry-haired man with ruddy cheeks was out in the yard when they arrived, two collie dogs close on his heels. He clapped Ben on the back by way of a welcome. 'And you must be the famous Ellie we've heard so much about. I'm Julian London.' Much to Ellie's surprise, he clapped her on the back too, leaving her feeling more shaken than ever.

'It's lovely to meet you,' she said. One of the collie dogs snaked its body between Julian's legs and nudged Ellie's hand with its head, clearly looking for some affection.

'We can do the niceties later, when my wife Caroline will tell me off for being rude, but right now we've got an emergency on our hands.' Julian ran a hand through his hair. 'It's Maisie, Ben;

she's kicking up blue murder because I've got to take one of the ewe lambs off her for slaughter.' Without another word, Julian stalked off towards the nearest of the barns with the two collies in hot pursuit, Ellie and Ben following on behind.

'Who's Maisie?' Ellie asked. 'One of the ewes?' She didn't like the idea of being the one to separate a lamb from its mother for the final time, and she slowed her pace as Ben laughed.

'No, Maisie's my goddaughter. She's six years old, going on thirty, and heaven help us all if she's screaming blue murder.'

Julian had already disappeared inside the double doors of the barn by the time Ellie and Ben had crossed the yard. A very determined voice could be heard arguing her point as they followed him in.

'Daddy, you can't take Holly! You promised you wouldn't take any of the lambs I fed. You pinkie promised!' The little girl's voice was high-pitched and she was clearly on the edge of tears.

'Yes, but I didn't know at the time she'd have a damaged stifle joint. She won't be able to have lambs of her own, Maisie, and you know we can't keep animals as pets on the farm. Even the dogs have to earn a living.'

'But I've been feeding her for ages. She knows me.' Maisie turned tear-filled eyes towards them. 'You agree, don't you, Uncle Ben? It would be cruel to send her away from the farm to *you know where*.' She whispered the last few words as though she was worried the sheep themselves might overhear and be upset.

'Well I agree with your dad that you can't have sheep as pets on a working farm just because you feel sorry for them.' Ben crouched down beside his goddaughter, who by now was openly sobbing. 'And it's time to stop feeding her too. She's more than twelve weeks old, and the lambs who weren't rejected by their mums were weaned a long time ago.'

'But that's the whole point! Even her

mummy didn't want her. We found her under a holly bush — that's why I called her Holly — and all of the other girl lambs I fed are getting to stay on the farm.'

'So they can have lambs of their own.' Julian threw his hands up in the air and whispered an aside to Ben and Ellie. 'I've only ever let her hand-feed the ewe lambs rejected by their mums, and kept the rams separate so she didn't have the upset of them going off to market. But I didn't realise this lamb was going to end up a hopalong.' Maisie's hearing was far too good though.

'What if *I'd* been born with a limp, Daddy? Would you have sent me away from the farm too?' She might only be six, but she was already an expert at manipulation, with her bottom lip sticking out and a look of desolation in her eyes.

'Of course not.' Julian sounded worn out, his argument running out of steam, but Ellie knew it would be really hard for him to back down. If he did, he could end up with a whole flock of unproductive sheep by the time Maisie was old enough to leave home.

'Hetty, Hilda, Hilary and Hermione all get to stay,' Maisie said. She threw her arms around one of the sheep in the pen next to her, covering its ears with her hands. 'But you're sending Holly for the chop!'

'We named them all with the letter 'H' after finding Holly,' Julian offered by way of explanation, and Ellie nodded. She hadn't missed the mention of the name Hilary, wondering if it was another sign. If she'd had doubts about what she'd been thinking of, that was enough to convince her.

'How much would you get for Holly at market?' Ellie turned towards Julian, aware of Maisie's eyes on her as she spoke.

'About £80, give or take, depending on the weight.'

'How about if I matched that to take Holly off your hands?' Ellie turned to smile at Maisie, who was regarding her with an air of suspicion.

'You're not going to eat her, are you?' The little girl tightened her grip on the lamb.

'No, I could take her back to my farm and she could keep my goat Dolly company.' Ellie moved a step closer to the pen and rubbed the lamb's soft black head. Holly had long since lost the prettiness of newborn lambs, but she had the same mournful look in her eyes as Gerald, and Ellie could imagine the two of them getting along just fine.

'You've got pets on your farm?' Maisie shot her dad an *I told you so* sort of look.

'Yes, but mine's not a working farm like this. It's a sort of retirement home for donkeys and other animals, and we're hoping we might start having weddings there soon too.' Ellie smiled as Maisie nodded sagely in response.

'Sounds like a much nicer farm than this one,' Masie said. Finally releasing her grip on the lamb, she hopped over the fence of the pen and slid her hand into Ellie's. 'Can Uncle Ben's friend buy Holly, Daddy? Please?'

'If Ellie really wants to waste her money on a good-for-nothing ewe, then I'll not stand in her way.' Julian gave another shrug of his shoulders, sneaking Ellie a quick thumbs-up sign when he knew Maisie wasn't looking. Everyone was happy, and Julian had been able to save face. Giving in to his very determined daughter was clearly a precedent he wanted to avoid.

'That's settled then, and you can come and visit Holly any time you like,' Ellie said. She was nearly knocked backwards as Maisie released her grip on her hand and threw herself into her arms instead.

'Really? I'll come all the time, then. Uncle Ben can bring me. Mummy says you're his girlfriend.' Maisie giggled as she said the word and Ben nodded.

'That's right, Maisie,' Ben said, 'and I promise to take you to see Holly as soon as she's settled in. She'll love it at Ellie's farm.'

'Well, what a blessing that's all sorted.

We'll get dinner before midnight after all.' Julian lifted Maisie out of Ellie's arms and hoisted her onto his shoulders. 'Let's go and see how Mummy's getting on with dinner while Ben checks over the rest of the ewe lambs.'

After Julian and Maisie left the barn, Ellie had another look at Holly. She was definitely lame, but otherwise she looked fine — like any other sheep, in fact — and she had a powerful bleat on her that might even give Gerald's braying a run for its money.

'Did you invite me up here because you know I'm soft-hearted and wouldn't be able to refuse a little girl or an injured lamb?' She turned to Ben, who slipped his hand into hers, much like Maisie had.

'No, I had no idea that any of the lambs Maisie was bottle-feeding were due for slaughter. I suspect that Julian was the one manipulating us — well, more me, really. I think he wanted me to tell Maisie from a vet's point of view that it was kinder to put Holly down.

After all, he had no way of knowing how kind you are.'

'Kind, or gullible?' She turned to look up at him.

'Definitely kind. No question about it.' Then he kissed her, leaving her in no doubt at all that he meant every word.

★ ★ ★

Dinner with Julian, Caroline and Maisie was enjoyable, if a bit chaotic. Julian agreed to deliver Holly to her new home the next day; and so it was that the menagerie at Channel View Farm grew by one more. Now all they needed was a way to pay for the upkeep — but the wait for the much-anticipated official brown envelope with the council's decision went on.

8

Holly settled into life on the farm extremely quickly and soon acquired a new second name that also began with an 'H'. Holly Houdini was an expert escapologist, capable of squeezing between the narrowest of gaps in the post-and-rail fence. Even with a lame back leg, within a week of arriving on the farm she'd twice managed to navigate the stile and get onto Alan's land. Thank goodness they were all now friends.

Holly and Dolly the goat were in the paddock next to Gerald's and they would often lean across into one another's fields, like neighbours chatting over the garden fence. One Saturday morning, Karen and Ellie were doing the morning rounds at the farm, checking on the animals, and had headed down to the bottom paddocks. Gerald saw them coming and began braying, Dolly bleating in unison with him; but there was no sign of Holly.

'Looks like she's disappeared again.' Karen grinned at Ellie. They'd both grown fond of the newcomer, who seemed to have inherited some of Maisie's wilful ways, and she hadn't strayed too far in her little adventures. 'I'll give Alan a ring and see if she's turned up over there.'

Ellie couldn't make out much of the one-sided conversation her mother was having with their neighbour, but one thing was clear: Holly hadn't escaped to Crabtree Farm this time.

'You don't think she could have fallen down the cliff edge, do you?' Ellie was suddenly gripped by panic. What would Ben say if the sheep was badly injured? More to the point, how would Maisie react? The little girl was due to visit later that afternoon, and Ellie could just imagine her face if her beloved Holly was nowhere to be found or, worse still, was lying at the bottom of the cliff. Dashing to the other side of the field, Ellie peered over the cliff edge and onto the beach below. There was no sign of Holly, thank goodness.

'What about the woods?' Karen turned towards her daughter, a look of panic suddenly crossing both their faces. Getting her mobile out again, Karen had another hurried conversation that Ellie couldn't quite pick up on. 'Alan's going to check the woods on his side and we can have a look on our side. She can't have gone far, can she? After all, it's not like people wouldn't notice a sheep walking down the middle of Kelsea Bay High Street. Especially not on a Saturday morning, what with it being market day.'

They ran down to the woods, Ellie by now convinced that Holly would be lying in a heap somewhere, and that the only thing worse would be having to tell Maisie. The search in the woods proved fruitless, too. The only animal life they saw was a rabbit — which shot into the nearest hole as soon as it caught sight of them — and a couple of squirrels scampering along the branches high above their heads.

Ellie felt a bit like Bear Grylls as she tracked Holly, looking for sheep droppings or some other sign to give them a clue to the direction in which the animal had gone. She wanted to call Ben, but it was hardly a veterinary emergency and a big part of her didn't want him to know that she'd lost the sheep.

Karen caught hold of Ellie's elbow after they'd spent at least half an hour searching for Holly to no avail. Karen's mobile had gone at one point and Ellie's heart had soared, hoping it would be Alan saying that the runaway sheep had arrived after all. It *was* him, but only to ask if they'd had any luck, as there was no sign of Holly in the woods on his side of the fence either.

'Do you think we should go back to the house and call the police?' Karen said.

'I don't think they'll send out an officer for one lost sheep.' Ellie's throat was tight from calling out for Holly, not to mention the emotion that gripped her every time she thought of having to face Maisie when she arrived later. 'Maybe we could give Daisy and Ben a call and ask them to spread the word, in case Holly has wandered down the road and is currently working her way through someone's prize marrows on their allotment.'

They headed back to the house, Ellie half-hoping that Holly would be waiting for them up at the yard, on the lookout for a bucket of sheep nuts or whatever treat she could get. Dolly the goat would eat absolutely anything, but Holly wasn't far behind her in the gastronomic stakes. The yard was totally empty, though, and even five minutes of rattling a bucket of Holly's favourite food didn't bring her running from her hiding place. Ellie knew she wasn't on the farm. If she had been, she wouldn't have been able to resist the lure of sheep nuts.

She gave in and rang Ben as soon as she got inside the house. He'd know what to do. 'It's me,' she said. 'Have you finished morning surgery?'

145

'I've just seen the last patient.' He was running the surgery without her as receptionist, since he only saw a few emergency patients on Saturdays anyway. 'Is something wrong?'

'Why does something have to be wrong?' Ellie gripped the phone. They might have only been together a few months, but he already knew her better than Rupert had. Perhaps it was because Ben actually listened.

'I can hear it in your voice,' he said.

'Holly's missing.' Ellie bit her lip. Stupid to get so attached to a sheep, especially one that spent all her waking hours trying to escape, but she couldn't help it.

'Again? Don't worry, she'll just be over at Alan's.' His tone was soothing, but he had no idea how long they'd already been searching.

'He's been looking everywhere on his farm too. There's no sign of her anywhere.'

'Do you want me to come up?' She could hear him already jangling his keys in the background as he spoke.

'If you can. But can you spread the word around town first, and ask Daisy if she can put the word out too? Maybe someone else will have seen her.' Ellie bit her lip again. 'What do you think Maisie's going to say?'

'Let's not worry about that until we have to, okay?' Ben was still using soothing tones. 'I'll go and see Daisy, then I'll be straight up.'

★ ★ ★

Every time there was a noise on the gravel in the yard, Ellie jumped up and looked out of the window, hoping it was going to be someone bringing Holly back. It had been the postman the first time, bringing a pile of letters she didn't even glance at and that she'd just put on the kitchen window. The bills could wait until later. The second time it was Ben, arriving in his truck to help with the next phase of the search.

'Are you okay?' He gave her a hug, and she just wanted to lean on him and not have to worry about tracking down Holly. She was worn out from working long hours at the surgery and doing whatever she could on the farm in between, even helping her mother out with some of the deli orders. Her repertoire was far more limited than Karen's, but she could whip up a mean Victoria sponge cake and flaky pastry that was light and crisp. Trying to spread herself between three jobs was hard, though, and she was starting to wonder if they'd ever hear from the council about the venue licence. She didn't want to think about how much of Daisy's big day was hanging on the outcome; the disappearance of Holly was enough to worry about for now.

'I've had better days,' Ellie said. 'I keep thinking about how upset Maisie's going to be.'

'We've got a while yet, and if the worst comes to the worst, we can always distract her with Gerald, Dolly and the others.' He gave her a half-smile, but they both knew there was no fooling

Maisie. 'Let's go and have another look. She can't have gone that far.' He passed Ellie her jacket as a light but persistent drizzle began to run down the windows outside, then turned towards her mum. 'Are you coming as well, Karen?'

'I'll wait here in case anyone tries to call the home phone.' She frowned, obviously feeling as helpless as her daughter. 'I don't suppose you happen to know what Maisie's favourite biscuits are, do you?'

'Gingerbread, and they're bound to help distract her.' Ben slung a comforting arm around Ellie's shoulders. 'Not that we'll need it. We'll be back soon, with Holly in tow. She might even have broken into her own paddock. I wouldn't put it past her.'

'Me either.' Ellie shrugged into her jacket as Ben removed his arm from her shoulders, and followed him out of the house. Two hours later, they were wet through, but there was still no sign of the runaway sheep.

By the time Ben set off to pick Maisie up at three o'clock, the sun had come out. Holly was still on the run, and for once Ellie wasn't looking forward to the sound of Ben's car on the gravel. Like all the things you dread, Maisie's arrival came too soon, and the tooting of Ben's horn meant there was no chance of pretending she hadn't heard them arrive. Deciding that the best thing to do was to just get it over and done with, Ellie headed outside, leaving her mother to put the finishing touches to the gingerbread men she'd baked for Maisie.

'Holly!' Maisie flung her arms around the sheep, who was standing nonchalantly in the middle of the yard, looking like she'd been there all day and completely oblivious to all the fuss she'd caused.

'Where did you find her?' Ben silently mouthed the words to Ellie, who just shook her head.

'Does she get to wander around and

do what she likes all the time?' Maisie turned towards them, her face shining as she was reunited with her favourite lamb.

'No,' Ellie said, 'she's usually in the paddock with Dolly. But as this was a special occasion, we thought she'd want to be here to greet you.' She crossed her fingers behind her back. This was the okay type of lie to tell; one that protected the children and kept the magic alive, like Santa Claus or the tooth fairy.

'She looks really happy, and she's even got a friend!' Maisie pointed to what looked like a ball of fur lying on the ground just behind Holly. As she spoke, the furball moved and a little brown head emerged. It was a small dog — some kind of terrier — and as it struggled to its feet, Ellie could see how fat it was. The dog waddled forward and Holly gently nudged it with her head, pushing it towards where Ellie stood.

'Hello, little one,' Ellie said. 'Where did you spring from?' She knelt down and stroked the dog's ears.

Maisie gave a little sigh. 'She's probably lost. I bet Holly told her how kind you are to animals and that's why she's here. Animals can talk to each other, you know. I read it in a Dick King-Smith book.' It wasn't the kind of logic you could argue with, and Ellie couldn't help smiling at the thought. Wherever Holly had been on her adventure, she seemed to have made friends with the little stray dog along the way, and perhaps Maisie's explanation wasn't so wide of the mark. Either way, the dog looked like it could do with Ben's attention.

'Shall we put Holly in the stable for a bit? You can give her some sheep nuts later, once her lunch has gone down.' Ellie could only imagine what the sheep had been stuffing her face with since she'd escaped, and she wasn't about to take any chances; a stable with two bolts and a padlock seemed like the best place for her.

Ben scooped the little dog into his arms. 'Sounds like a good plan to me. And Maisie can demolish some of

Karen's gingerbread whilst I take a look at this chap. Then we can all have a tour of the farm. I'm keen to see if Gerald looks well enough to make the fund-raiser.'

*   *   *

Ben came into the kitchen ten minutes later with the little brown dog still tucked under his arm. 'Well, one thing was immediately obvious when I took a proper look. He's a she, and she's very pregnant — about to give birth any day, I'd say.'

'I've made her a temporary basket.' Ellie pulled a cardboard box out from under the table. It was lined with blankets, and the little dog set about making herself a bed as soon as Ben put her inside.

'It looks like she might already be nesting,' he said.

Karen looked at Ben. 'Don't we need to find her owner, then? She'll want to be at home, with the people she knows looking after her.' She looked concerned, but Ellie knew it was nothing to do with her being worried about getting saddled with yet another unwanted animal.

'By the looks of it, I don't think anyone's been taking proper care of her for a very long time,' Ben said, taking the drink Karen had poured for him.

'See? I told you Holly had brought her here. She knew you'd look after her.' Maisie had been busy colouring in a large sheet of paper that Ellie had given her, but she didn't miss a trick. A knock at the door made the little dog's ears prick up and she started to shiver, clearly a nervous wreck.

'That'll be Alan,' Karen said. 'I told him about Holly . . . ' She caught herself just in time. ' . . . waiting out in the yard for Maisie to arrive. He said he'd pop over for a cup of tea to celebrate. He doesn't even know about the dog yet. It's been quite a day!'

Moments later, Karen ushered Alan into the kitchen. He shook hands with

Ben and gave Ellie a warm smile, listening intently as Karen explained about the little dog. Peering into her basket, he rubbed his chin with one hand as if he was trying to remember something.

'I might be mistaken, but I'm sure I've seen this dog before. I kept hearing yapping in the night last week, and when I looked out of my bedroom window toward the caravan park, there was a little terrier like this chained up to one of the caravans. I complained, but the manager said he'd sort it and not to worry, as the people who'd been staying there were moving on the next day anyway.' He sighed deeply. 'I wonder if they left her behind.'

'If they did, you can bet your life they did it on purpose.' Ben had a murderous look on his face, and for a moment Ellie was taken back to the first day she'd met him, when he'd been so cross about the state that Gerald was in.

'Well, we'll keep her tonight.' She looked at her mother, who nodded swiftly in response. 'But then we ought to try and find out who she belongs to, just in case someone is desperately looking for her.' Glancing at the dog, Ellie suspected that Ben was right. Sadly, the little terrier didn't look well-loved. 'Unless, of course, you think she'd be better off at the surgery.'

'No, she'd be shut up in a cage there. This way we can keep an eye on her if she shows more signs of going into labour.' Ben smiled at her. 'I suppose we'd better give her a name, for tonight at least.'

'What do you think, Maisie? What's a good name for a lost dog?' Ellie looked across the table at the little girl's drawing, where she'd added a sheep that was a remarkably good likeness of Holly and a little brown ball of fur which was unmistakably the dog now curled up a few feet away from her.

'I think Ginger would be a good name. She's almost the same colour as the gingerbread men that Karen made for me, and she turned up on the same day.'

'Ginger it is then.' The little brown dog lifted up her head as Ellie spoke. It was as good a name as any, and Ellie already had the feeling the dog might end up staying far longer than the one night they'd agreed to. Whatever knack it was that Aunt Hilary had for finding and taking in the waifs and strays of the animal kingdom, Ellie seemed to have inherited it.

★ ★ ★

Ben took Maisie home at seven o'clock, by which time she'd been around the farm three times, completed the almost impossible task of plaiting Gerald's mane, and thought up names for seven boys and seven girls to cover all eventualities with Ginger's puppies. She'd also fed Holly some sheep nuts and brushed her coat with an old dog brush until the lamb resembled a giant powder puff.

Karen invited Alan to stay for dinner, and Ben was coming back to join them after dropping Maisie off. They were all on puppy watch, waiting to see if Ginger's digging at the sides of her cardboard box really was a sign that puppies were on the way.

They had an enjoyable meal together, and were playing cards afterwards when Ginger started to pant much more strongly. Ben told them it was best not to interfere with her unless it looked like she was getting into trouble, so they watched from a safe distance as five puppies emerged. There was one ginger one, two jet-black ones, and a couple of tabby-looking ones that were a mixture of several colours. The identity of the puppies' father was destined to remain a mystery, but clearly he hadn't been the same breed as Ginger. When Ben was sure that there were no more puppies to come, he checked them over. There were two males and three females as it turned out, and they were all feeding well within an hour of being born. Ginger might not have been well looked after during her pregnancy, but she was doing a pretty amazing job of being a mum.

Alan put a hand on Karen's arm as she stood up to put the kettle on, and reached down inside the rucksack at his feet. 'This calls for a proper celebration,' he said. 'None of your tea malarkey. I brought a bottle of champagne over when you told me about Holly turning up. Only, it didn't seem appropriate to open it while Maisie was here, especially with her not knowing about the sheep escaping in the first place. It's been in the cupboard for years — I can't even remember what it was bought for originally. But champagne only gets better with age, or so I'm told.'

'Alan, you never cease to amaze me!' Ellie planted a quick kiss on his cheek and he beamed in response. She had a suspicion he might become a permanent fixture one of these days; he was like an adoring puppy himself when Karen was around. Much to her surprise, Ellie found herself liking the idea more and more. Alan was one of the good guys, and that was what her mum deserved.

'I'll get the champagne glasses,' Ellie said. 'Sit down, Mum. Alan's right, this definitely isn't a time for tea.' As she crossed the kitchen to the cabinet where they kept the glasses, the pile of post she'd propped up on the window sill hours before caught her eye. She picked it up and dropped it on the table, placing the champagne glasses beside it, and a brown envelope slithered out from the middle of the pile.

'Look at the franking — it's from the council,' Karen said. 'It'll be the results of the inspection.' She picked up the envelope, turning it over carefully in her hands before handing it to her daughter. 'You should be the one to open it. It's you who put all the hard work into this.'

'I don't think I can.' Ellie ran a finger along the flap sealing the envelope. It would be so easy to rip it open and read what was inside — the council's verdict on whether Channel View Farm would make an appropriate venue for civil wedding ceremonies. Yet there was so much riding on it, so many of her dreams, that she was sure the words would swim in front of her eyes even if she was brave enough to read it. 'Can you do it, please?' she asked Ben.

A bit like pass the parcel, she handed it to him. He peeled back the envelope slowly, like a presenter on an awards show, and Ellie had to sit on her hands to stop herself from snatching the envelope out of his grasp and tearing it open. The anticipation was killing her.

'They've granted the licence!' Ben had a huge grin on his face, but Ellie still made him repeat it three times before it finally sank in.

'Well, I don't know about you, but I think there's more cause to open this champagne than ever.' Alan carefully released the champagne cork, muting it with a tea towel so as not to frighten Ginger or her puppies. As they raised their glasses, he made a toast. 'To the Chapmans of Channel View Farm and their new venture.'

Karen raised her glass a second time, making what Ellie had suspected official. 'And to Ginger, the newest member of the family,' she said, beaming at Alan.

9

By the time the summer fundraiser for the church hall and Elverham animal sanctuary came round, Gerald was in rude health. His coat was shiny — as much as an old donkey's coat ever could be — and Maisie had plaited his mane again for the occasion. Ellie was also taking Dolly down to the green that ran parallel with the sea wall, where the fundraiser was being held. She'd decided it was too risky to take Holly Houdini down with them too. If the lamb slipped her lead rope, she could disappear in minutes, which would cause panic in the crowd. Knowing Holly, she would also steal everyone's picnic lunches and knock down the hotdog stand if it got in her way.

Ben was bringing some guinea pigs who needed a new home, as well as his own dog Humphrey, a black-and-white

Great Dane that stood nearly as tall as Dolly. They would be asking for a 10p donation for people to pet the animals of their choice, and Ben would be doing a talk on animal care. Karen and Alan had offered to help out, but since her mum had already baked several cakes for the tea tent, Ellie was keen for her to have a day off and just enjoy the fundraiser.

By three p.m. the old ice-cream tubs, which they'd used to collect the donations, were brimming with coins. When someone dropped a £10 note into the tub without saying anything, Ellie looked up into the face of the last person she'd expected to see.

'Rupert!' She put a hand on Gerald's neck to steady herself. 'What on earth are you doing here?'

'I came to see how country life was treating you.' He looked her up and down in the way that had always made her feel so self-conscious, as if he was actively searching out her flaws. 'It obviously suits you. You look really well.

Slimmer.' The bottom line for Rupert clearly hadn't changed, and Ellie felt herself relax. He was part of her old life; and, seeing him, she was more certain than ever that she'd done the right thing in moving to Kelsea Bay.

'I've left you a few messages,' she said. 'I wanted to return your ring, but I never heard back.' She was vaguely aware of Ben standing a few feet away, talking to a couple about the importance of considering very carefully what would be the right pet for their child.

'I noticed you weren't wearing it.' Rupert sounded surprised.

'What did you expect? We broke up months ago.' As Ellie spoke, she could hear the pace of Ben's speech quickening too. He was clearly keen to get away from the couple to find out what was going on. Ellie had shown him a picture of Rupert once when she'd been throwing out some of her old things, not long after she'd moved to the farm. Ben must have recognised him from the photo. She'd have wanted to be in on

165

the conversation, too, had their roles been reversed.

'I didn't *expect* anything.' Rupert moved to take her hand but she snatched it away. 'I suppose I hoped you might have missed me, though, and that you might have changed your mind.'

'And are you telling me that you'd be willing to move to Kelsea Bay if I had?' Ellie laughed as Rupert pulled a face. Absolutely nothing had changed. She knew what motivated him. She was just an acquisition that had got away, which made him want her all the more. He was the same with properties he had his eye on — she'd seen it time and again. It was a pointless conversation, anyway. She felt nothing for him anymore.

'It must be hard work up at the farm, making ends meet,' he said. 'It looks like it needs a lot of upkeep.'

'Looks?' She was surprised by his choice of words. As far as she knew, he'd only ever met Hilary a couple of times, and he'd never visited the farm. By the time he and Ellie were together,

Hilary had banned anyone from visiting her there. 'Have you been up there, then?'

'I drove by on the way down here.' He gave a casual shrug but didn't meet her eyes. Something wasn't ringing true.

'Well you obviously didn't get a proper look, because we're doing just fine. In fact we had some really exciting news last month — we've been approved by the council as a wedding venue, and we've got our first wedding at the beginning of September.'

'Lovely.' Rupert's mouth formed the word, but there wasn't a trace of sincerity in it. It was probably his idea of hell, getting married on a farm, surrounded by animals who had seen better days. They'd never got as far as agreeing on a venue for their own wedding, but it would have been sleek, modern and soulless if Rupert had got his way; Ellie knew that now. It was funny, looking at someone you thought you'd loved for years and realising you'd never really known them at all.

'I'll call you about meeting up.' He paused, searching her face, as if waiting for some sort of sign that she still had feelings for him. 'We can sort out the ring then, if you really want to give it back.'

'That would be good. It'll wipe the slate clean.' Ellie held out the £10 note that Rupert had dropped into her ice-cream tub; there was no such thing as a donation without strings, as far as he was concerned. But he shook his head.

'See you soon, Ellie.' Turning on his heel, he disappeared into the crowd, leaving her with a distinct feeling of unease.

Seconds later, Ben slid an arm around her waist, having finally escaped from the clutches of the couple who had been trying to decide between a guinea pig and a rabbit for their children. 'Was that who I think it was?' He pulled her in closer as she nodded. 'It looks like he gave you a generous donation.'

'He'll be after something in return.' Ellie sighed. She didn't want her old life coming to Kelsea Bay, so the sooner she could return the ring and make a final break from her ex-fiancé the better. 'Nothing's ever as straightforward as it seems with Rupert. He didn't come all this way just to say hello.'

'If you walked out on me, I'd go to the ends of the earth to find you.' Ben's lips brushed against her cheek, and she knew that he would. Rupert couldn't hurt her anymore, because she didn't need his approval; she didn't want it, either. She'd call him in the week and get the ring couriered back to him. She had Ben now — someone who wanted her just the way she was — and that was a million times better than anything Rupert had ever given her.

★   ★   ★

'You could have bought half a dozen coconuts for the amount of money you've spent trying to win one.' Karen laughed as yet another one of the small red balls that Alan had aimed went wide of the mark.

'That's not the point!' He was laughing too. 'I wanted to win one for you, and it's all for charity in any case. If I'd just wanted to buy a coconut, we could have nipped to the supermarket and been home before lunch.' He hurled the last of the three balls forward without really looking, and this time it made contact with the coconut. It wobbled for a bit, and for a horrible moment Karen thought it was going to stay put, before it finally toppled onto the grass below the stall.

'Bullseye!' Alan swung her round in a circle — something no one had tried for years, much less achieved. He didn't even make a groaning sound as he lifted her off the ground. Years of building up muscles farming had obviously paid off.

'If this is what you're like when you win a coconut, remind me never to be around if your lottery numbers come up. I don't think my spine could take it!' Karen gave a little curtsey as he handed her the coconut. 'Why thank you, kind sir. I'll treasure it forever.'

'Actually, I was hoping for some coconut macaroons, so we'll have to smash it open at some point.' Alan grinned. 'But in the meantime, can I interest you in a visit to the tea tent?'

'Always. You know me.' Putting the coconut into her handbag, Karen linked her arm through his.

There was a brass band playing outside the tea tent, and several people walked past with what Karen recognised as slices of her cakes on their plates. It still gave her a warm glow inside to think of people enjoying something she'd baked, especially when she saw someone smile in satisfaction as they tasted the first forkful.

Alan pulled out a seat for her at one of the small garden tables that had been set up outside the tent. 'Do you want something to eat?'

'No, thanks. I'm saving myself for the coconut. Just tea would be lovely.'

'I'll go and queue up, if you promise to save me a seat.' He squeezed her shoulder and she turned to look at him, wanting to say something significant; something about always saving him a seat next to her. But she still felt shy sometimes, as if she might be pushing this quiet man faster than he really wanted to go. Any movement in their relationship had always been on his terms; and as much as she wanted to tell him how she felt, it was less scary this way.

Several groups of people drifted past as Karen sat waiting for Alan. She was starting to recognise many of the locals from Kelsea Bay, some of whom she'd been introduced to when she'd been delivering her cakes to the deli. She could also see Ellie across the green, chatting animatedly to the children who were petting Gerald. The old donkey looked perfectly content to be the centre of attention, even if he did occasionally have a rummage with his nose in someone's pocket or a conveniently open handbag that happened to pass him by.

Karen smiled. Ellie had settled well

into the community. Working at the veterinary surgery with Ben had helped, and she'd embraced local events like the barn dance too. She was a natural networker, and now that she was out of Rupert's shadow she was blossoming, on the cusp of starting her own business.

Almost as soon as Rupert's name had entered Karen's head, she saw him. There was no mistaking him, standing bold as brass on the other side of the tea tent and chatting to Daisy, who couldn't keep anything to herself if her life depended on it. By now Rupert would know everything that Ellie had done since she'd arrived in Kelsea Bay. But the important question was what Rupert was doing here. Like her daughter less than half an hour before, seeing Rupert again left Karen with an uneasy feeling.

'Sorry it took so long.' Alan set the tea tray down on the table, with two mismatched cups and saucers and a plate of shortbread that clearly wasn't homemade. 'The queue stretched right round the inside of the tent, and by the time I got there all the good stuff — and by that I mean everything you made — was long gone.'

'Never mind. There's always the coconut macaroons to look forward to.' She put her hand over his, pushing thoughts of Rupert out of her mind. She wasn't going to let an unwanted visitor spoil a perfectly lovely afternoon.

'You're always making things for me, so I'd like to give you something in return.' Alan's voice had dropped in volume, as though he was worried someone might overhead.

'Don't be daft — you've done far more for me than I ever could for you. All the things you've helped us with, and building that beautiful gazebo. It's stunning now that it's finished.'

'I built it for you.' He was stumbling over his words a bit. 'I mean, with you in mind. I wanted it to be the perfect place for you to choose, if you ever wanted to get married again.'

Karen gave a nervous laugh. 'Who'd ever want to marry me?'

'I would.' He cleared his throat, nerves seeming to get the better of him. 'No, scratch that — I mean I *do*. I do want to marry you. I wish I could be one of those people who made a big show of things by asking the brass band to play 'Isn't She Lovely' while I dropped down on one knee, but I'm just not like that. I've hidden something under the shortbread instead.'

Karen picked up three biscuits before she saw it — a gold ring in the middle of the plate, set with rubies in the shape of a flower, and a cluster of diamonds in the centre.

'I . . . ' She was totally speechless for a moment; but when she looked at Alan there was only one answer. 'Yes!'

10

'Are you sure you're not rushing into this?' Ellie didn't look up at her mother as she spoke; it was taking all her concentration to keep the paint inside the heart-shaped outlines on the metal jug she was decorating. There were ten centrepieces to prepare for the tables at Daisy's wedding. In the high after getting the go-ahead for the venue, it had seemed like a good idea to hand-paint them. Now, struggling to decorate only the third jug, she was definitely starting to wish she'd bought them online.

'Maybe it seems quick because we've known each other slightly less than six months. But I've been on my own for twenty-five years, Ellie, so I'm not prone to rushing into things.' Karen was busy, too, as she spoke; when Ellie eventually looked up at her, she was folding green fondant icing over little square cakes.

The preparations for Daisy's hen night were turning out to be almost as time-consuming as co-ordinating the wedding itself.

'You weren't on your own. You had me.' Ellie put the paintbrush down for a moment. Her hand had started to shake with the effort of keeping it steady.

'And that's all I ever needed. But when you got engaged to Rupert, I realised that one day very soon you'd be moving on with your life, and you wouldn't want me holding you back. I've been lucky to have you at home with me for far longer than most mums do, and we've always been close, but I'd have hated for you to come to resent that. When we inherited the farm and you decided to finish things with Rupert, it meant we had time together again. I know you don't like me making assumptions about Ben, but even if you two don't end up together — ' She shot Ellie a look that suggested she thought otherwise. ' — one day you'll want to settle down to a life with your own family. Meeting Alan has been like a second chance at love for me. I'll never regret marrying your dad, because we had you; but I know what it's like now to have someone put you first, and I've never had that before.'

'But I do. You've always put me first.' Ellie smiled, her worry that her mum was rushing into the engagement with Alan lifting off her shoulders. 'It's about time someone did that for you, and there's no denying he's a lovely man.' She picked up the paintbrush again. 'It looks like I'm going to have to get a bit better at painting these hearts. With your wedding on the cards, we've suddenly got a rush on.'

'There's no hurry for us, and we're certainly not about to steal Daisy's thunder.' Karen rolled out another piece of green icing. 'You and Ben might even beat us yet.'

'Mum! How many times do I have to tell you?' The tip of the brush slipped as Ellie protested, making the last of the hearts look distinctly wobbly; this was definitely going to be relegated to a position in the darkest corner of the marquee.

* * *

Surprisingly for Daisy, she was having a very relaxed hen night. They were using the seating area in the deli as the venue, and she was having a meal for family and close friends. At the bride-to-be's request, Karen had made some cakes for the party, the little square ones she'd decorated earlier. Half of them were covered in green fondant icing, with a large daisy in the centre, and the other half had little houses on top to represent Nathan's job as an architect. They were like a prequel to the wedding cake, and each one was a miniature work of art.

One of Daisy's friends leant across the table, nearly knocking over her drink in the process. 'So are you going to tell us about the wedding dress?'

'Let's just say the big day is all about

me. Everything from the flowers to the cake is daisy-themed!' She giggled and took another sip of champagne. 'And if it wasn't for these ladies — ' Daisy swept her hand in the direction of where Karen and Ellie were seated, at the far end of the table. ' — I would never have got my dream wedding. If Jamie finally gets round to asking you to marry him, Pru, I can't recommend them enough!' Daisy, who was exuberant even without the aid of several glasses of champagne, could probably have been heard three streets away.

'I'll bear that in mind.' Poor Pru looked distinctly deflated, and Ellie immediately felt sorry for her. It must be hard having a friend like Daisy, who was the life and soul of every occasion. Ben never seemed to feel the need to compete with his sister, though. He was full of life, but in a less obvious way, never trying dominate the conversation or make sure he was the centre of attention. He wanted to hear Ellie's opinion on things, which was like a breath of fresh air after Rupert. She'd tried calling her ex again after he'd turned up at the fundraiser, but Rupert hadn't returned her calls. It was odd, when he'd gone to all the trouble of coming to Kelsea Bay, and she just wished he'd show his hand and tell her what he was really after.

'Time for a song, I think!' Daisy, who by now had drunk the best part of a bottle of champagne, got to her feet. 'Just because I decided not to go dancing for my hen night, it doesn't mean we can't have some fun. Ellie, can you put on track thirteen please?' She gestured towards the iPod docking station that was linked into the deli's sound system. They usually played classical music — apparently it made the customers buy more, or so Daisy had said — but there were obviously a few of the bride-to-be's other favourites on the iPod for occasions such as this.

'All done for you.' Ellie smiled at her friend as she selected the requested track. 'Take it away!'

'I'd like to dedicate this song to my wonderful fiancé, Nathan Hardy!' Daisy began to join in with the track. It was a love song, but one Ellie wasn't familiar with; and even if she was, the way Ben's sister was murdering the tune would have made it difficult to recognise. She could see people walking past the window in the glow of the streetlight above, most of them stopping to see where the caterwauling was coming from and smiling at the sight of Daisy in full swing. Ellie's mouth went dry as a familiar figure paused outside the window. It was Rupert, and he was looking straight at her.

* * *

'If that's *Kelsea Bay's Got Talent*, then I think you need to draft in some singers from a neighbouring town.' Rupert smirked, but Ellie didn't even attempt to laugh at his joke. Daisy was still inside the deli, launching into a second tune, but it had taken all Ellie's powers of persuasion to convince Karen not to follow her outside to confront her ex.

'What are you doing here again, Rupert? If you're so desperate to get your ring back that you've taken to hanging around Kelsea Bay on a regular basis, why don't you just answer my calls?'

'I don't want the ring back.' He took a step toward her and she took two steps back. 'It's a promise to wed, and people should always keep their promises.'

'It's over, Rupert, and please don't come here pretending to be heart-broken. It's been months, and we've both moved on.' She turned to leave, but he caught hold of her wrist.

'Well I know *you* have. The local vet, isn't it? I was speaking to his sister at the fundraiser. It's a breach of contract, you know, breaking an engagement, and nothing good comes of breaching a contract.' He smirked again. 'You want to be careful with that little business of yours — people don't take too kindly to broken promises. Daisy's clearly got high expectations, and it would be a real shame if you couldn't fulfil them.'

'Are you threatening me, Rupert?' She pulled her wrist free.

'Just a warning from a friend, that's all.' But the look on his face was anything but friendly, and Ellie had a horrible feeling this wasn't the last she'd see of him.

*   *   *

'I've couriered the ring back to his office and tracked the delivery online. It's been signed for, so he's definitely got it back. There's no reason for him to come back here again.' Ellie spoke to Ben through gritted teeth, gripping drawing pins between them as she stood on a ladder and hung swaths of organza from one of the beams in the barn. Ben was holding the ladder steady. Even taking into consideration that it was his sister's wedding, he'd been amazing in offering so much help to get Channel View Farm ready for its very first ceremony. Thankfully, his receptionist had made a full recovery from her back injury, and so Ellie had been relieved of all duties at the surgery. Every time Ben was free, he was up at the farm, assisting with the preparations for what was shaping up to be the wedding of the year.

'Do you think it was really the ring he was after?' Ben's warm voice drifted up to where Ellie was perched at the top of the ladder, stretching to position the last pin so it couldn't be seen. 'I saw him coming out of one of the estate agents' offices on Tuesday with a stack of property details. You don't think he's planning to move here to be closer to you, do you?'

'Ha!' Ellie nearly dropped the drawing pins she was holding. 'He didn't want to come near the farm when we were together. He's just trying to intimidate me because I was the one who broke things off. The property details will be for his job. He's an acquisitions director for a large development firm. You want to tell Julian to watch out, or they'll be turning his farm into a spa and luxury hotel before you can say sheep dip.'

'He'd have to get past Maisie first, and good luck to him with that!' Ben put his arms up to steady her as she descended the last few steps of the ladder, and she turned round to face him when she reached the ground.

'Now that the ring's back,' he said, 'we can draw a line under the whole thing, and celebrate the launch of the business and your mum's engagement properly. Everything's coming right for you, Ellie, and I think your great-aunt must be up there somewhere orchestrating it all.'

'I hope so.' She rested her head on his shoulder, praying that he was right. If Rupert really was determined to get his own back, they'd need all the help they could get.

* * *

With less than forty-eight hours to go until the wedding, Ellie was working her way through the checklist. Ben had helped her finalise the decorations in the Old Barn, where Daisy and Nathan would be signing the register and all the official paperwork would be completed to make things legal. It would also be the backup venue for the ceremony itself, if the weather finally broke and the glorious summer they'd been enjoying suddenly disappeared, making a wedding in the gazebo out of the question. Ellie had bought a hundred gold chairs after getting the licence from the council, which could be moved from the Old Barn to outside the gazebo, depending on where the couples chose to marry. Alan had put the use of a tractor and trailer at their disposal, so that the chairs could easily be moved from one end of the farm to the other. Daisy and Nathan were only having sixty guests, so it wouldn't be quite such a military operation to move the location for their ceremony if the need arose. That said, Ellie had been keeping an almost obsessive watch on the weather, and so far it looked as if Saturday was going to be a good day.

The Elverham Marquee Company were coming to erect the reception venue the next day, just twenty-four hours before the wedding, and it would be dressed with flowers early on the day of the wedding itself. As Daisy had said on her hen night, the flowers would be daisy-themed, and they would be on everything from the place cards to the confetti that was going to be scattered on the tables. Ellie had eventually managed to paint all of the old milk jugs with hearts; these would also be filled with daisies, and placed as the centrepieces on each of the ten tables. Daisy had said she didn't want a top table, so they were having ten tables of six instead, including one for the bride and groom and their parents. The cake would be put out on display at the same time as the flowers, so that everyone could admire it as soon as they entered the marquee. Everything had been thought out to the tiniest detail, including the positioning of an air-conditioning unit, to ensure that neither the marquee nor the pièce de résistance — the wedding cake, covered in hundreds of icing-sugar daisies — got too hot.

Karen had finished the cake a few days earlier and had almost completed the handmade chocolates — not surprisingly, in the shape of daisies — that were going to be put in miniature cake boxes and used as favours on the tables. There was no chance of anyone forgetting the bride's name at this wedding! Having done so well with her side of the arrangements, she had gone into Kelsea Bay to make the last of the deliveries to the deli before the big day.

And so it was, late on the Thursday afternoon, that Ellie found herself alone at the farm, double-checking that everything that could have been made ready for the wedding, was; and that anything else that needed doing was properly planned. She was just making a note to put up some parking signs for the guests when the familiar sound of tyres on gravel made her look up from the list. Either her mother had turned into Lewis Hamilton, and could now get to town and back in twenty minutes, or Ben had finished work at least two hours earlier than expected, or they had a visitor.

She knew whose car it was as soon as she saw it. The look-at-me bright red sports car was so Rupert, it could have been designed just for him. Gerald must have heard the throaty exhaust right down from the bottom paddock, as Ellie couldn't miss the frantic braying once the noise of the engine had cut out. Even Ginger jumped up from her bed. Her brood of puppies, who would soon be ready for homes of their own, immediately followed suit, yapping at the unwelcome interruption to their afternoon nap.

'What?' Ellie got to the door before Rupert had a chance to knock. There was absolutely no need for him to be here now. She'd sent the ring back, with a note apologising and wishing him luck for the future. It was time for him to leave her alone.

'Is that any way for you to greet your fiancé?' He produced a bunch of flowers from behind his back like a half-hearted magician's act.

'You're not my fiancé.' Slamming the door in his face was extremely tempting, but this had to be resolved once and for all.

'Ex-fiancé, then. For now at least.' His foot was already in the door, anticipating that she might change her mind and slam it after all. If he ever lost his job, he'd make a darn good double-glazing salesman.

'There's no 'for now' about it, Rupert. I just want to know what you want, so you can get on with your life and leave me alone.'

'I suppose you want me tell you out here, on the doorstep?' He pulled a face that suggested he thought she was being completely unreasonable, and the urge to shut the door on him almost overwhelmed her, but she knew it would just make things more protracted. He was definitely after something, and once he had got what he wanted he'd be on to the next thing and out of her life.

'Come in, then. You've got five minutes. I'm supposed to be working, finalising the plans for the wedding on Saturday.' She stepped to one side and flinched as he brushed past her. Her life with him seemed light years ago.

Going straight through to the kitchen, he picked up her list. 'Doesn't all this wedding-planning make you think about what might have been?'

'You'd have organised the whole thing, Rupert. Told me what to wear and exactly how much weight I needed to lose before the big day.'

'That's not fair.' He looked straight at her. 'I was only trying to help you.'

'I'm fine as I am. Happier than I've ever been. I've got a great place to live, my dream business, and wonderful family and friends. I don't need your advice.' She crossed her arms over her chest to make the point. 'Or anyone else's.'

'I haven't come to give you any advice.' He sat down without invitation. 'I'm sorry if I sounded threatening the other day. I was just desperate to make you see that we shouldn't have thrown everything away. We might have had a few problems, a few things we needed to change, but it didn't all have to end. I miss you, Ellie. I want things back the way they were, and I want to come and live here on the farm with you. If that's what it takes to win you back.'

'Are Ant and Dec going to pop out from behind a cupboard in a minute and tell me that I'm being pranked?' Ellie leant against the sink unit and waited for him to start laughing; to say it was all a big joke. 'You're telling me that's why you're really here? What about all your trips to the estate agents? I thought you were here for work.'

'My, my, Kelsea Bay is a town full of nosy little parkers, isn't it? Well, I'm afraid your spies have got it wrong,

Ellie. I was looking for a house to rent, in case I couldn't persuade you to give us another go straight away. Somewhere I could stay, close by, while we got to know each other all over again.'

The thought made Ellie shudder, and she still found it hard to believe that love — however deluded — was at the core of Rupert's motivation for anything. 'That would be a bad idea,' she said. 'It doesn't matter how long you hang around; I won't change my mind.'

'It's the wedding that's got you talking like this; making you stressed.' Rupert smiled, but his eyes were dark and slightly menacing. 'I'm sure I won't need to rent anything long-term. Just give me seventy-two hours. The hotel in town is fully booked from tonight, but let me stay here until the day after the wedding — and if I haven't convinced you by then, I promise I'll get out of your life for good.'

'You can't stay here, but if it's what it takes to get you to accept that it's over, I'll give you your seventy-two hours.

There's somewhere close by you can stay. But I'll want it in writing that if I don't change my mind, it's the last time you'll come here.' She was already reaching for a piece of paper.

'If you like. After all, I'm not the one who breaches their promises, and I'm sure you'll have seen the light by the day after the wedding. You wouldn't want to break my heart before then, would you, Ellie? It wouldn't be good form for your first-ever wedding booking to be ruined by your heartbroken ex-fiancé turning up on the big day and causing a fuss.'

If that wasn't a threat, then she didn't know what was, and Rupert was perfectly capable of delivering on it. If he didn't stick to his side of the bargain after the wedding, she'd call the police and get an injunction if she needed to. Right now she'd play along. If it kept Rupert quiet for a few more days, and meant Daisy's wedding went off without any drama, then it would be worth it.

'Here, sign this.' She shoved the piece of paper towards him, on which she had written a few lines outlining his promise. It would be something to show the police, at least: proof that Rupert was well aware he was harassing her with unwanted attention. 'While you're doing that, I'll ring and book you a caravan at the holiday park next to Crabtree Farm for the next two nights.'

'A *caravan*?' Rupert looked up from signing the paper, horror at the suggestion written all over his face.

'You'll survive.' Ellie picked up the phone and added under her breath, 'More's the pity.'

11

The morning of the wedding dawned bright, just as the forecasters had promised. Every sound in the night had woken Ellie up, and she'd had to keep peering out of the window to make sure the marquee was still there and hadn't been blown into the Channel by some freak storm. Rupert hadn't been near on the day before the wedding, so the marquee had gone up without distraction and everything was going according to plan. The caterers had dropped off the food for the buffet, and every spare inch of space in the two new fridges Ellie had bought for the business was taken up with their platters. The florists had been in to dress the marquee and the Old Barn, and had also left a large display of daisies, which were due to be moved to the gazebo on the cliff top just before the ceremony. They weren't taking any chances with a last-minute change to the weather. It was all going perfectly — too perfectly, as it turned out.

Karen had gone down to the bottom paddock, with Alan driving the tractor and trailer, to set the chairs up for the wedding ceremony once they were convinced that a freak thunderstorm was very unlikely to break out after all. Her scream a few moments later carried all the way up to the house, and Ellie ran out and straight down towards the gazebo, in only her socks. Terrified that something awful might have happened — and half-expecting to see the tractor lying on its side with Alan pinned underneath — she was shocked to see everything looking perfectly normal, except for the fact that all of the bottom paddocks seemed to be empty.

'Someone's cut the chains on the gates for both these fields!' Karen exclaimed. 'All the animals are gone, even Gerald!' She was gasping and shrugging off Alan's attempts to comfort her. 'He was Aunt Hilary's favourite; if anything happens to him . . .'

Ellie felt surprisingly calm, having expected to be met with a scene of devastation. 'It'll just be some kids, thinking it's a laugh to let them go. No one is going to steal our motley collection of animals. An ancient donkey, a goat with ADHD and a lame sheep aren't high up on the steal-to-order list. The three of them will just have gone to the nearest source of food and stopped there.'

But almost as soon as the words were out of her mouth, Ellie's heart sank towards her shoe-less feet. The marquee . . . it was filled with flowers and — oh, God — the wedding cake. It was like she was in one of those cartoons where she was running without actually moving. She must have been, though, because as she got closer to the marquee she could make out the outlines of shapes inside, then the unmistakeable sound of a bleating goat. Maybe they hadn't touched the cake after all. Consumption of the flowers would be a disaster, but a small one in comparison to the demolition of the pièce de résistance.

Sadly, as she finally got to the entrance to the marquee, any last vestige of hope disappeared. Gerald and Dolly both had their heads buried in the ruins of Daisy's wedding cake, and Holly was wandering around with half a dozen daisies hanging out of one side of her mouth, every single centrepiece having been upended; and almost all of the flowers were gone.

'No!' Ellie shouted the word and held on to the single syllable for what seemed like an hour. It might not have been as long as that, but it was enough time for Karen and Alan to make it to the marquee by the time she finally stopped.

Alan spoke first. 'I'll get the animals back to the field.' It was a practical suggestion, but it didn't begin to cover what needed to be done to put things right.

'Oh Mum, what are we going to do?'

Ellie picked up a piece of squashed wedding cake as Alan led Gerald out of the tent. There were strands of grass and half-chewed daisies all mixed up with it.

'I've got a cake for a Christening next week,' Karen said. 'It's the same shape, but it's only got plain white icing on it. I don't know what we can do about the daisies, but it's something.' She sounded almost as shocked as Ellie was. They'd put so much work into everything, and she'd wanted it to be so right; not least because it was Ben's sister who was getting married, and Ellie loved him so much. It was a funny time to realise it, standing in the middle of what looked like the devastation from a small earthquake, but she knew it was true. There was no one else she wanted to be with more at that moment, with his arms around her, telling her it would all be okay. But the thought of letting him or his family down soon had hot tears burning the back of her eyes.

'The wedding is only four hours

away, and there's no time,' Ellie said in a choked voice. 'Look at the centrepieces. And Maisie's headdress was here as well, but that's gone too.' She bit her lip, fighting a losing battle to keep the tears at bay. Ben was due to bring Maisie to the farm an hour before the wedding so she could get ready. She was a bridesmaid, and Daisy had decided that Maisie's parents, Julian and Caroline, couldn't be trusted to get her to the ceremony on time. Apparently Julian had been late to his own wedding after one of his sheep had managed to get herself wedged in a ditch. The florist had left Maisie's headdress in the marquee, saying that the air-conditioning should help the daisies stay looking fresher for longer. Of course, they hadn't reckoned on them coming into contact with Holly.

'I can call the ladies from the deli,' Karen said. 'It's been closed for the day for the wedding, so they've got the morning off to get ready, but I'm sure they'll be prepared to spend a bit less time on their hair and make-up if I explain it's an emergency. Luckily, daisies are one of the easiest flowers to make out of icing. If I can show the girls how to do it and get a little production line going, whilst I work on recreating Nathan's cottage, we might just about do it in time.' She was already reaching for her mobile, and Ellie had more respect for her mum than ever. She'd always been able to cope, making sure the bills were paid and giving Ellie a worry-free child-hood, despite her dad not being around. And here she was again, not panicking, but working to put everything right and make sure Ellie was okay.

'Shall I ring the florist whilst you're doing that?' Ellie had to get a grip and follow her mother's lead, but she didn't hold out much hope that the florist would somehow have over-ordered on wild daisies and be able to come and replace everything that Holly and her chums had devoured.

'Were all the flowers daisies?' Alan was back in the marquee, clipping a lead rope onto Dolly this time.

'Yes. The biggest displays are in the barn, but all the centrepieces will need redoing,' Ellie said. 'There were bunches of daisies in all of the jugs. We need some to go in the gazebo, too, and some more to make Maisie a replacement headdress. Why couldn't Daisy have chosen something easier to get hold of, like roses or lilies?' She blinked back the tears again. Crying wasn't going to help anyone.

'I know where we can get hold of plenty of wild daisies.' Alan put a hand on her shoulder and the urge to cry subsided. This must be what it was like having two parents to look out for you. 'I might need some help with the picking, though. So maybe you could ring round and see if you can get some volunteers for that?'

*   *   *

An hour later, a small army had been mustered, and operation wedding recovery was underway. The community in Kelsea Bay had rallied round, and it looked like the dream wedding might just be back on after all.

Ben popped his head around the corner of the marquee just as Ellie was putting the last of the centrepieces back in place. 'How are you getting on?' he asked. Alan had pulled off a small miracle finding so many wild daisies, and if anything they were prettier and far fresher than the originals. She'd opened her mouth to ask him where he'd got them from, in the midst of thanking him profusely, but her mum had put a finger to her lips and Ellie had got the message. She'd hear the story eventually, but the look Karen had given her suggested that now wasn't the time.

'I think we're almost there,' Ellie said. 'I just need to sort out Maisie's headdress — although I should probably prioritise my own bird's nest first.' She made a vain attempt to flatten down her hair, which was suffering the effects of the mad dash they'd had to try and put everything right. 'Did you and Alan manage to finish things up at the gazebo?'

'We did, and Alan's still up there now, keeping Maisie entertained while I came to check on how you were doing. I can't believe the change in him since he met your mum. He's helping Maisie finish off plaiting Gerald's mane again. If they can manage that, maybe you should let them have a look at yours!' Ben laughed and Ellie couldn't help joining in. So she might look like something the cat had dragged in, but the marquee looked beautiful; and judging from the laughter coming from the kitchen, her mum's gang of willing helpers were getting on well too.

When Ben had arrived at the farm with Maisie in tow, Ellie had hastily explained about the animals escaping. He'd just kissed her, telling her it would all be okay and asking what he could do to help. She should have known there'd be no reproach from him, just support. She wanted to tell him what she'd realised earlier — that she loved him, but it wasn't the time. All hands on deck was the only way to describe it, but they'd pulled together, about fifteen people in total making up her mother's chain gang and Alan's team of flower pickers.

'There's a princess bridesmaid out here all ready to get into her gown,' Alan called out from the yard. Ben took Ellie's hand and led her out into the sunshine.

'Never mind a princess — she's a miracle worker if she did that to Gerald's mane!' Ben laughed. The old donkey look distinctly unamused to be sporting short sticky-up plaits threaded through with daisies. Maisie, on the other hand, looked as pleased as punch.

'He's so pretty, don't you think?' Ellie said. 'I wanted to make a daisy chain for Holly too, but Alan said we hadn't got time. He did put all the flowers around Gerald's head collar, though.'

'He looks beautiful, sweetheart. And if we can't manage it ourselves, maybe Alan could help with your headdress too. He's done such a good job with Gerald's head collar.' Ben took hold of Maisie's hand just as Karen and some of her helpers emerged from the kitchen to have a look at Gerald's makeover.

'My goodness!' Karen laughed, her cheeks flushed red — no doubt a result of how hard she'd been working for the last few hours. 'Aunt Hilary would have loved to see this. She would have laughed herself hoarse.'

Ellie crossed the yard and folded herself into her mother's arms. 'Thanks for everything, Mum. And I don't just mean the cakes.'

'No need for thank-yous, love. We're a team.' Karen stroked a hand across Ellie's unruly curls. 'We're a bigger team these days, though.'

'And all the better for it.' Ellie cuddled closer to her mum as the girls who'd been helping in the kitchen crowded around Alan and the donkey. 'I'm going to help Ben get Maisie ready and grab a quick shower, but can you thank Alan for me? He's been amazing. If I had any doubts about you rushing into things with him, there's not a trace of them left.'

'I will, and that means a lot to me, too, Ellie. You've earned the right to enjoy this wedding, and you're all the more likely to do so if you're dressed up for the occasion. I can sort out the last few bits down here.'

★ ★ ★

'Did you really decorate his head collar like that?' Karen took Alan's hand as they looked across the stable door at Gerald. For safety's sake they'd decided to put the old donkey, the goat and Holly Houdini into the stables. A repeat of the morning's events was more than any of them could bear to think about.

'Maisie said it spoilt the look of his mane when I put the head collar on.' Alan grinned. 'She's quite a character, that one. I just threaded a few daisy stems through the buckle and eyelets, that was all.'

'Don't make light of everything you've done today or over the last few months, Alan.' She squeezed his hand. 'I know you find it hard to take compliments, but you'd better get used to it. Ellie wanted me to tell you how grateful she is too.'

'I'd do anything for the pair of you. When you first arrived, I was so angry, thinking you'd come in to strip Hilary's place bare and that you'd turn out to be like everyone else — just in it for yourselves.'

'Seeing everyone working together today, you surely can't still think that most people are just out for themselves? Look at how many people have given up their time to help us.' Karen turned to face him. 'It restored my faith, anyway.'

'You're right, but I've only seen that thanks to you. You've made me feel like part of a family again; part of a community. Mind you, if I ever find out who let those animals out today and put you and Ellie under so much stress,

I won't be responsible for my actions.' He brushed his lips against hers for a split second. 'Now go and get ready. I'm expecting a dance later, and the sight of Alan 'Crabby' Crabtree on the dance floor will cause even more of stir than Gerald's fancy hairdo. People will have to start seeing that I'm a changed man at some point, though. And it's all down to you.'

12

Ellie was ready with minutes to spare. Ben had once more come to the rescue, saying it was part of his role as usher to make sure the guests knew where to go once they'd parked their cars. Groups of guests were already thronging around the gazebo, chatting and laughing before they took their seats. Champagne glasses were lined up on a table in the barn, ready to toast the happy couple as they signed the register. Gerald was serenading all the arrivals with enthusiastic braying, and the wedding cake mark II had been put back in position in the marquee. It was difficult to believe that only a few hours earlier everything had been chaos.

When the vintage Rolls-Royce pulled up with Daisy and her dad in the back, even Gerald had the grace to stop making so much noise and look inquisitively over the stable door. The bride was wearing an antique dress with a pattern of daisies fashioned from lace, while her dad was sporting a large daisy in his buttonhole. Even Daisy's tiara had the little flowers picked out in diamante.

Thank goodness they'd been able to replace the cake and all the centrepieces in time, as not having daisies there as well would have been so obvious. Ellie had hardly had a second to think about who had let the animals out, but while she followed the bride on a slow walk towards the gazebo, she saw the severed chains that had secured the gates to both paddocks now hanging loose. Her theory that it had been children playing a prank suddenly seemed far less likely. Whoever had done it would have needed some heavy-duty bolt cutters to get through the links. She'd stepped up security following Holly's numerous escapes, and letting the animals out of the fields was no longer an easy task, so it definitely couldn't be done accidently.

For a moment, thoughts of Rupert flitted into her mind. He'd been ominously quiet since his visit two days before. But it couldn't be him. He hated animals for a start, and what would he have to gain from letting them escape? If he'd wanted to impress her, he could have shown up and 'found' them or helped out after the demolition derby that ensued — that would have made more sense. As it was, the deadline for him changing her mind about the engagement was fast approaching. She was certain now that she'd never really loved Rupert at all. She wasn't in the business of deliberately hurting anyone's feelings, but she'd happily tell him that, if that was what it took to completely break free.

By the time Daisy and her father reached the gazebo, with Maisie just behind, all the guests had taken their seats and were turning to witness the arrival of the bride. Daisy had asked Ellie to book a harpist. It was strangely hypnotic hearing the sound of the 'Wedding March' played like that. As Ellie caught Ben's eye, tears threatened for the second time — only this time they were happy ones.

It really was a stunning place to get married; everyone said so. There was a buzz of excitement about it, once the service was over and the guests were following the newlyweds back to the barn for the signing of the register and yet more photographs. Ellie was asked if she'd consider hiring out the barn and a plot where a marquee could be pitched for a ruby wedding anniversary, as well as a twenty-first birthday party.

The guests' reactions to the centrepieces and Karen's amazing wedding cake were exactly what Ellie had hoped for, too. At least ten people asked if the flowers on the cake were real, and the stack of business cards that she'd discreetly placed on a small table in one corner of the marquee at the base of yet another jug of daisies had all been taken.

There'd hardly been a chance to speak to Ben all evening. As the wedding co-ordinator, Ellie had to keep an eye on everything; so just being a guest, like everyone else, wasn't an option. She was determined to manage at least one dance with him, though.

He held her close as they moved around the dance floor. It was the first time they'd ever danced together, and Ellie wasn't disappointed. She'd seen some fairly awful dancing and some attention-seeking moves, not least from the bride herself. But Ben could dance. Alan had been a revelation earlier, too, looking surprisingly light on his feet as he'd led Karen around the floor. Ellie had a funny feeling that it wouldn't be long before she'd be helping her mother organise a wedding. As much as she'd promised Ellie she wouldn't rush into it, anyone with half a brain could see that Alan and Karen were made for each other, so why wait?

'So how's your first wedding experience been?' Ben asked her as they continued to dance slowly.

'My first wedding has been . . . exhausting, terrifying and amazing — all at the same time. What does it look like from the guests' side of things, do you think?'

'It's gone without a hitch. Except for those of us who know, no one would have a clue what kind of drama went on in this tent this morning.' He stroked her hair as he spoke.

'I owe you a favour. In fact, I owe half of Kelsea Bay a favour.'

'Funny you should say that. I've been tasked with decorating Daisy and Nathan's car, and I wondered if you'd give me a hand? I know your duties as wedding co-ordinator don't stretch that far, but I thought perhaps you'd do it as the girlfriend of the bride's brother instead.'

She liked the way he said that; it almost made her sound like part of the family. 'It would be my pleasure, Mr Hastings, and I know just where I can lay my hands on a can of silly string. I'll meet you in the yard in ten minutes.'

★　★　★

Ben stood back to admire their handiwork. 'I know I've said it already, but you really are a miracle worker! Where did you get all this stuff?'

'I had a hunch it might all still be in the loft.' Ellie put the finishing touches to another daisy design on the back windscreen. 'Aunt Hilary used to go all out for Christmas when I was younger. She had snow spray in every colour and used to spray pictures onto all the windows in the farmhouse. Plus, she liked a silly-string fight as much as the next person. I used to have so much fun visiting her here; it was an amazing place to be as a kid.'

'I'm sure Maisie thinks the same, and you've been her idol ever since you saved Holly from being turned into lamb chops!'

'That's good. She's a lovely girl. It sounds like we've pulled off decorating the car just in time, too.' Ellie grinned as the DJ made an announcement from inside the marquee. 'Apparently the bride and groom are about to leave for their honeymoon.' She led the way back into the tent. It had been a great wedding to start the business with. Daisy had wanted it to be traditional, with the bride and groom leaving before the party ended and everyone waving them off. It might just have been another way for Daisy to ensure that she was the centre of attention, but Ellie liked the idea anyway.

'Right — get ready, ladies; I'm going to throw my bouquet!' Daisy was already standing in the middle of the black-and-white checkerboard dance floor with her back to the rest of the guests. 'One, two, three!' She hurled the bouquet of wild daisies over her shoulder, and they sailed past most of the guests' heads — landing, whether he wanted them to or not, straight in Alan's arms. Six months before, he would probably have thrown them right back; but as it was, he seemed to enjoy his own few minutes in the spotlight, joking that he'd be picking out a wedding outfit any day before presenting the bouquet to Karen.

There was a flurry of congratulations and kisses as the bride and groom bid farewell to their guests, most of whom followed them outside to give Daisy exactly the sort of send-off she'd been after. She clapped her hands with delight at the sight of Nathan's almost unrecognisable BMW decorated with daisies made from multicoloured snow spray and what looked like a thatched roof of silly string.

'It's brilliant, Benji, you clever old thing!' She threw her arms around her brother's neck and it took him a moment or two to break free.

'It's all down to Ellie. She's a wedding co-ordinator like no other. She can even lay her hands on silly string and snow spray in every colour of the rainbow without a moment's notice.'

'In that case,' announced Daisy to anyone within earshot, 'I think she's officially a keeper.'

'I hope so.' Laughing, Ben submitted to yet another of his sister's hugs. 'And I promise I'll keep you posted.'

'You do that! And as for you, young lady . . . ' Daisy turned her attention to Ellie. 'You've given me the best darn wedding ever. I know I'm demanding, but I also knew you could pull it off. That's why I wanted *this* wedding, and for you to organise it, so much. It's also why I couldn't bring myself to book anywhere else. After all, why settle for second best?'

It seemed that in every pivotal moment Aunt Hilary had a hand in things. Daisy's words took Ellie right back to that day down at the paddock when her great-aunt had explained why she'd never wanted anyone but her lost fiancé. Ellie hadn't understood it back then, or even when she'd got engaged to Rupert. It was only in the last few weeks that it had really begun to make sense, and it was perhaps the most important of all the legacies Hilary had left.

★　★　★

The party had gone on for a couple of hours after the newlyweds had set off, and it had been far too late to start the clean-up operation by the time the last of the guests left. Alan and Ben had both headed home a little after midnight, with a promise to return the next morning and help get everything straight again, in exchange for one of Karen's famous cooked breakfasts.

By the next morning, Ellie had received several texts congratulating her on organising such a fantastic wedding. She'd read the latest just as Ben arrived and slid the phone into her pocket as she went to the door, bringing him straight through to the kitchen.

'Tea?' She'd been assigned the duty of making drinks, with Karen at her usual place in front of the cooker, whipping up bacon, sausages, three variations of eggs (scrambled, poached and fried), mushrooms, tomatoes and fried bread. Offering the relatively simple options of tea, coffee or orange juice seemed like the good end of the deal to Ellie.

'I could murder a coffee actually.' Ben's warm brown eyes crinkled in the corners as he gave her a rueful smile. 'I stayed at my parents' place last night, and Mum wanted to sit up half the night talking about the wedding and how brilliant it was. You're everyone's favourite wedding planner, by the way.' He smiled again as she handed him a strong cup of coffee. 'I can hardly keep my eyes open as a result. And then some boy racer in a red sports car nearly ran me off the road on the way up here. Maybe it was my fault; I was probably still half-asleep.'

'Did you see the driver's face?' Ellie had gone cold at the mention of the red sports car. She'd almost been able to forget about Rupert when the wedding had gone so well, but she was fully expecting him to turn up. After all, today was the deadline he'd set himself to change her mind.

'No. It all happened so quickly.' Ben shrugged. 'Still, no damage done.'

'Can I get you another drink, Alan?'

Ellie poured tea into his mug as he nodded. A typical farmer, despite the late night the evening before, he'd been up at the crack of dawn and had already moved all the chairs back down from the gazebo and made sure everything down at that end of the farm had been cleared away. They just had the tent to tidy up, ready for the Elverham Marquee Company to dismantle after lunch, and a few things to put straight in the barn. All in all, Alan was worth his weight in gold.

Ben took a seat next to the older man. 'How are you feeling this morning? Have you recovered from catching that bouquet yet?'

'Just about. And I wouldn't put your wedding suit back into mothballs just yet, because I'm trying to persuade Karen to make ours the second Channel View Farm wedding.'

'Thats brilliant! Congratulations.' At the very moment Ben shook Alan's hand, there was a loud braying from the yard outside.

Ellie smiled. 'Sounds like Gerald

wants to join in with the congratulations too. Either that or he's reminding us he's been shut in the stables since yesterday morning.'

'I wouldn't put it past him, after getting a taste for wedding cake yesterday, to be giving his breakfast order.' Karen put a large plate of food in front of Alan as she spoke and the old donkey brayed again, as if in agreement.

'Are you sure that's just Gerald? I thought I heard a scream.' Alan put down his knife and fork and they all listened. For a moment there was nothing, and then the unmistakeable sound of someone shouting out for help.

Much like when Karen had screamed the day before, Ellie shot out of the house with nothing on her feet; only this time she was headed across the gravel and into the yard, instead of down the path and onto the grass. The stones digging into the soles of her feet slowed her down, so that by the time she reached the stable, where the shouting seemed to be coming from, Alan and Ben had already beaten her to it.

'What the hell are you doing here?' It was Ben who'd spoken, and Ellie had never seen him so angry; not even on the day they'd met, when he'd been so upset about the condition Gerald was in.

'Never mind what I'm here for! Get this donkey off me. I've got a good mind to sue you when I get out of this stable. He's had me trapped in here for ten minutes, and every time I try to get past him he goes to kick me, or bares those ugly yellow teeth of his.' The voice was unmistakable, the attitude even more so. Rupert.

'Sue us?' Alan thundered. 'You're the one who's trespassing, being on this land! Never mind what you're doing being in there with the donkey.' He pulled himself up to his full height as he spoke. He was a big man, and it seemed he could still call upon his old persona if he needed to. 'If you're who I think you are, then you're definitely not welcome here.'

226

'I think Ellie should be the judge of that.' Rupert spoke in a whining tone; Gerald still had him hemmed into the corner of the stable.

'I've told you before that I don't want to see you again, Rupert,' Ellie said flatly. 'In fact I made you promise that after today you wouldn't come here again.' She tried to keep her voice level, but Rupert's behaviour was so erratic that she was scared of what he might do next. She couldn't bear the thought of Gerald getting hurt in the fallout.

'You said you'd give me your answer today, about us getting back together. It's what I came here for.' Rupert clearly wasn't going down without a fight, and Ben shot Ellie a look. She knew what he must be thinking, but she shook her head. She'd explain later and tell him that she hadn't wanted to jeopardise Daisy's wedding, and just hope he understood.

'The answer's always been the same, Rupert. I don't love you, and I know now that I never really did.' She hadn't wanted to say it, but he was hardly playing fair, and it was just as important for Ben to hear it as him.

'Ellie's told you how it is,' Alan said. 'But you coming to the farm to talk about that doesn't explain what you're doing here in the stable.' He reached inside the open top half of the stable door and flicked on a light switch that illuminated all three stables. It was now much easier to see Rupert cowering in the corner, his back to the donkey who was indeed baring his teeth at the unwelcome guest. 'That rip in your jacket — how did you do it?' Alan's tone was forceful. It was obvious Rupert was going nowhere until he answered the question.

'Your filthy donkey probably did it!'

'I don't think so. Karen, come and have a look.' Alan made a space for her to stand next to him so she had a better view of Rupert. 'Does that coat look like the same material we found snagged on that branch when you thought someone was sneaking around the woods, watching the farm?'

'I'd bet my last pound on it.' Karen's eyes clouded over, as if she was beginning to piece it all together and didn't like what she saw. 'And that's not the only lie you're telling. Anyone normal would just knock on the door, not hide in the corner of a stable. What are you really doing here, and what were you doing in the woods that night? And don't give me any rubbish about it being because you miss my daughter so much.'

Rupert attempted to dart past the donkey, and Ellie spotted a yellow plant with distinctive finely divided leaves sticking out of his clenched fist. 'Is that ragwort?'

Ben vaulted over the stable door and had Rupert pinned against the wall within seconds, wrenching the plant out of his hand. Unbolting the door, Alan followed him in.

'We're finished playing your game now.' Ben's voice was shaking with anger. 'Answer Karen's question or I swear to God I won't be responsible for my actions. You know ragwort could have killed that donkey, don't you?'

'I don't know what you're talking about.' Rupert unclenched his fist, the ragwort falling towards the floor. As Gerald moved to investigate, Alan reached down and grabbed the plant, stuffing it in his pocket out of harm's way.

'Your sleight of hand wouldn't even convince the donkey.' Alan moved a step closer and Rupert's eyes flickered towards Ellie, as if he expected her to help. But she had to hear it; had to hear just how far he'd been prepared to go to get what he wanted.

'I didn't want to kill him. I just wanted to make him sick.'

'You're the worst kind of scumbag, do you know that?' Ben was almost growling.

'How about we do the same to you?' Alan looked more than capable of carrying out the threat. If Rupert had been scared of the donkey, he must be terrified by now. 'We could poison you. Just enough to make you sick, of course.'

'Look, you're overreacting.' Rupert

was wheedling now, trying to talk himself out of a difficult situation; but what he said next only made it worse. 'I was just trying to get Ellie to let go of the farm and come back to her old life. If the donkey got sick and I reported you to the RSPCA for not taking proper care of him, they might close this place down. I tried it the easy way at first, just letting the wretched things out to ruin the wedding; but that didn't quite go according to plan, thanks to all those sodding do-gooders who flocked up here at the last minute.'

'It was you?' Ellie looked at the man she'd once agreed to marry as if he were a complete stranger. 'But why would you want to ruin Daisy's wedding? You don't even know her.'

'It wasn't personal. I just wanted the business to fail so you'd give up the farm.'

'You're telling me all this is about getting Ellie back?' Karen's voice had an unmistakable edge to it as Rupert nodded in response. 'Then I'm telling you you're a liar. Why would you be lurking in the woods late at night, if that's what you really came for?'

'I promise you, that's all it was,' Rupert insisted. Ben kept him pinned against the wall as Alan moved closer, so that his face was only inches away from Rupert's.

'Promise me that *again*,' Alan challenged him, the consequences if Rupert repeated his lie unspoken but obvious all the same.

'All right, for God's sake. If it makes you back off I'll tell you. Whatever you choose to believe, I really did come to get Ellie back at first. I didn't take kindly to coming in second place to a farm.' Rupert inched his head to one side, trying to get further away from where Alan stood, watching his every move. 'But when I saw this place from the road, I knew it would be perfect for a holiday park. It's a project my company is trying to acquire a site for, and it seemed like fate — two birds with the same stone. I held off on coming to see Ellie while I did a bit more research.'

'And was it research that took you into the woods that night?' Karen demanded. Rupert nodded his head.

'I brought one of my company's surveyors down to look at the place, but I knew we'd have to do it under cover of darkness, since you're all so precious about this place. The stupidest part is that it could make you rich, at least in comparison to how you're living now, surrounded by flea-bitten creatures like this.' He eyed Gerald.

'It was about making *you* rich, though, wasn't it, Rupert?' Ellie's voice was shaking. 'You've never once thought about what I wanted in all of this, or mentioned coming here because you loved me. You just didn't want to lose.'

'None of us have to.' Despite his vulnerable position, something in Rupert just couldn't give up. 'All right, so the two of us are over. But you could still sell me the farm. Make a profit, get out of this back-end of nowhere and return to civilisation. They want to build a holiday park here with static caravans overlooking the sea, a swimming pool and club house — it'd be a gold mine, and they'd pay you well for it. There's nothing like it round here, only that little caravan place up the road. My firm bought that too, years ago, but holidaymakers want more than that now.'

'That was *your* firm?' Alan had drawn his arm back and Ellie moved to stop him, but Karen was quicker, slipping into the stable and catching hold of him with a split second to spare.

'He might be pure poison, love,' she said, 'but you can't blame Rupert for what happened to your place. It was before his time.'

'He's cut from the same cloth as them — just after what he can get.' Alan's fist was still tightly clenched.

'I know, but I also know he's not worth you getting in trouble for. I need you here, with me.' Karen's words had the desired effect, and slowly the fingers of Alan's hand uncurled.

'We're never going to sell the farm, Rupert, and I never want to see you again.' Ellie spoke slowly, making it perfectly clear she meant what she said. It had gone far enough; he'd told them the truth — at least as much of it as he'd ever reveal. And she knew her mother was right; Rupert wasn't worth Alan or Ben's trouble. He was her mistake, and she should be the one to sort it out. 'If you come back here again, I'll call the police.'

'Do that. I'll deny everything, and when they see the marks on my chest, it's your new boyfriend they'll be locking up.'

'And I've got this.' Ellie held up her mobile phone. 'I've recorded the whole conversation.' Something had made her hit the 'record' button when she'd seen him in the stable. Maybe it had come from knowing him of old, but whatever it was she was glad she'd done it.

'You can't do that, it's inadmissible!' Rupert was squirming again, cornered, and Ben kept his hands against the other man's chest.

'Then there's your coat,' Ellie said.

'More proof you were lurking in the woods and trespassing on our land.' Even as she spoke, she couldn't understand that. Rupert was so vain, it seemed strange he hadn't chucked the coat out straight away.

'I only wore it to blend in; to look like the rest of the charity shop rejects around here so I could make you believe I wanted this life.' He couldn't help himself; and if Karen and Ellie hadn't been there, he'd almost certainly have got what he deserved.

'But now we both know where we stand,' Ellie said. 'And I meant what I said — I've looked into getting a restraining order, and if you turn up here again I know exactly what to do.' She stared straight at Rupert, holding his gaze until he looked away. She had the power now. 'Let him go, Ben, please.'

Alan and Karen took a step back, and eventually, but clearly not wanting to, Ben followed suit. Rupert pushed past them, cannoning Karen into the donkey's side. Jerking his head up in surprise,

Gerald opened his mouth, sinking his teeth straight into Rupert's forearm.

'I should have killed that filthy thing when I had a chance!' Clutching the injury with his other hand, Rupert pushed through the gap in the stable door. 'The whole lot of you deserve each other! And don't worry — if I never see any of you again, it'll be too soon!'

Rupert was a bully, and he'd been given a taste of his own medicine. He wouldn't be back. Ellie could have gone straight to the police, but it wasn't worth it. Having him out of her life was victory enough. The sound of his sports car roaring up the lane from wherever he'd hidden it when he'd snuck onto the farm was like music to her ears.

'Thanks, Alan.' She turned towards the others. Alan nodded, his arm already around Karen. 'Ben, about what Rupert said . . .'

'It doesn't matter.' His words said one thing, but his face another. 'Look, I'm sorry — I know I said I'd stay and help clean up, but there are some things at the surgery I need to get sorted, and all this stuff with Rupert has taken up time I hadn't accounted for.'

'Okay.' Ellie reached out her hand, but he didn't move towards her. 'But can we talk later?'

'I'll call you if I finish in time.' He didn't meet her eyes, and it seemed that maybe Rupert had won after all. The sound of Ben's car roaring up the lane just moments later wasn't nearly as welcome a sound.

13

Ellie was glad of the distraction that getting the farm sorted out provided. She'd even offered to help pack the marquee tent away, but they'd said something about health and safety rules, so she'd been relegated to making tea. Alan had taken Karen out for Sunday lunch, their breakfast having been ruined by Rupert's arrival, and Ellie had been glad to let them go. Being around two people so obviously in love was made all the more difficult now that she didn't know where she stood with Ben. She could understand him being angry. Rupert had done his best to make it sound as though she still had feelings for him; that she was struggling to choose between him and Ben. But that had never been the case — there'd never been any contest. She just needed some time alone with Ben to make him understand.

Once the men from the Elverham Marquee Company had finally set off, with everything neatly packed up in the back of their lorry, Ellie was at a loose end. She toyed with ringing Ben or driving down to the surgery to speak to him, but he'd said he'd ring her when he was free, and making him talk before he was ready would probably only make things worse.

Instead she wandered down to the bottom paddock, where Gerald was still scraping his teeth against the almost bald ground of the paddock, blissfully unaware of his brush with death. Rupert hadn't reckoned on what he was up against, though. Gerald had been Hilary's favourite for a reason; he was made of tough stuff.

Ellie sat on the large flat stone at the edge of Gerald's paddock. The cliffs of France, just visible across the sea, were shrouded in a cloak of mist. It was the first week of September. Autumn was on its way, and already the leaves on the trees at the edge of the woods were turning to shades of orange and brown. It had been such a wonderful summer — almost perfect — but now it felt like everything was changing again.

'If you're up there, Aunt Hilary, can you just sort one last thing out for me? Make Ben realise I only said those things to Rupert so he wouldn't ruin Daisy's wedding.'

'He already knows.' The voice behind her almost caused her to fall off the rock.

'Ben, you nearly made me pass out!'

'I know, and I'm sorry. Sorry about scaring you, and sorry about overreacting so badly earlier.' He sat down next to her. 'It's only because of how I feel about you. I couldn't stand the thought that you might still have feelings for that . . . for Rupert.'

'I don't. I meant what I said — I never did; at least, not compared to the way I feel about you. These last few weeks have made me determined never to settle for second best again.'

She smiled. There was Aunt Hilary, making her presence felt.

'I love you, Ellie. You know that, don't you?' Ben kissed her slowly, which was greeted by a loud braying from Gerald. Laughing, he pulled away. 'And I think you might be trying to tell me you feel the same way.'

'I am, though Gerald seems determined to steal my thunder. I love everything about my life on the farm and in Kelsea Bay, but the best part of that is you.'

'And how about the name Hastings? What do you think of that?'

'It's something I could live with.' Ellie looked into his eyes. 'Forever, if the offer is there.'

'Forever sounds all right to me.'

As the mist closed in and an autumn chill filled the air, Ellie leant against his shoulder, the third Channel View Farm wedding already on the horizon.